"Stop Fighting Me, Mistral,"

he said huskily, taking in her furious, frightened expression. Her eyes flashed emerald sparks at him, but in their depths, shadows lurked, and her mouth was tremulous. "As much as I'd like to do otherwise, I promise that I'm not going to do anything that you don't want me to." He smiled ruefully. "It's been a long time since a woman told me no. It is…something of a novel experience."

"Well, in that case, I can't imagine what kind of women you've been hanging around with," Mistral snapped indignantly.

"I've been wondering that very same thing for quite a while now. I guess that's why I couldn't stop myself from kissing you, although I knew that it was too much, too soon." He gazed at her intently. "I would never do anything to hurt you, Mistral. I hope you know that."

"I don't know what to believe anymore…."

Dear Reader,

The perfect treat for cool autumn days are nights curled up with a warm, toasty Silhouette Desire novel!

So, be prepared to get swept away by superstar Rebecca Brandewyne's MAN OF THE MONTH, *The Lioness Tamer,* a story of a magnetic corporate giant who takes on a *real* challenge—taming a wild virginal beauty. THE RULEBREAKERS, talented author Leanne Banks's miniseries about three undeniably sexy hunks—a millionaire, a bad boy, a protector—continues with *The Lone Rider Takes a Bride,* when an irresistible rebel introduces passion to a straight-and-narrow lady…and she unexpectedly introduces him to everlasting love. *The Paternity Factor* by Caroline Cross tells the poignant story of a woman who proves her secret love for a brooding man by caring for the baby she *thinks* is his.

Also this month, Desire launches OUTLAW HEARTS, a brand-new miniseries by Cindy Gerard about strong-minded outlaw brothers who can't stop love from stealing their own hearts, in *The Outlaw's Wife.* Maureen Child's gripping miniseries, THE BACHELOR BATTALION, brings readers another sensual, emotional read with *The Non-Commissioned Baby.* And Silhouette has discovered another fantastic talent in debut author Shirley Rogers, one of our WOMEN TO WATCH, with her adorable *Cowboys, Babies and Shotgun Vows.*

Once again, Silhouette Desire offers unforgettable romance by some of the most beloved and gifted authors in the genre. Don't forget to come back next month for more happily-ever-afters!

Regards,

Joan Marlow Golan
Senior Editor, Silhouette Desire

Please address questions and book requests to:
Silhouette Reader Service
U.S.: 3010 Walden Ave., P.O. Box 1325, Buffalo, NY 14269
Canadian: P.O. Box 609, Fort Erie, Ont. L2A 5X3

REBECCA
BRANDEWYNE
THE LIONESS TAMER

SILHOUETTE *Desire*®
Published by Silhouette Books
America's Publisher of Contemporary Romance

SILHOUETTE BOOKS

ISBN 0-373-76171-6

THE LIONESS TAMER

Printed in U.S.A.

Books by Rebecca Brandewyne

Silhouette Desire

Wildcat #955
The Lioness Tamer #1171

REBECCA BRANDEWYNE

is a bestselling author of historical novels. Her stories consistently place on bestseller lists, including the *New York Times* and *Publishers Weekly*. She was the recipient of the *Romantic Times* Career Achievement Award (1991), *Affaire de Coeur's* Golden Quill Pen Award for Best Historical Romance and the Silver Pen Award.

For Jeanne and Curtis,
because we all went through the sideshow together.
In friendship and with much affection.

Prologue

Every Child's Dream
Chicago, Illinois
The present

"You're what?" Sophia Westcott stared at her tall, dark, devastatingly handsome son, stunned and incredulous, unable to believe her ears. Surely he was teasing her, she thought after a moment. Yes, that was it. He was having a joke at her expense. She began to laugh then, but when she saw that her son's black eyes did not twinkle mischievously, that his mobile mouth did not curve crookedly in an answering grin, the sound died away, and her hands fluttered nervously in her lap. "Jordan...you—you just can't be serious," she said, aghast.

"Mother, I assure you that I have never been more serious in my life," Jordan Westcott stated calmly before he flicked an imaginary piece of lint from the lapel of his tailored suit jacket. Then he glanced studiously at his immaculately clean fingernails, as though totally oblivious of the consternation his announcement just moments past had caused both his mother and his uncle, who were seated on the luxurious burgundy chesterfield in his penthouse office of Westcott International. "I'm running away to join the circus."

"Why, I—I never heard anything so ridiculous in my life!" Charles Westcott sputtered indignantly to conceal the guilt and shame that he felt. "I'll tell you what it is, Jordan. You've been working way too hard. The stress of running the family business since your father's untimely death has proved too much for you. You've finally snapped under the strain—and it's all my fault. I should have been more help to you instead of taking things easy…worrying about my old ticker and slipping away most afternoons to play golf."

"You're not to blame, Uncle Chas," Jordan insisted quietly but firmly. "You did what the doctor advised for your heart, which was the only sensible course of action. And I'm certainly not asking you to come out of semiretirement for my sake. There's no need whatsoever for that, and what's more, you know it. Together, you and Dad assembled one of the best management teams in the world to run Westcott International. Half the time, I feel like little more than a figurehead myself.'' The slightest trace of impatience tinged Jordan's voice at this last.

Ever since Richard A. Westcott, III, had been killed in a ballooning accident five years ago, Jordan had attempted to fill his father's shoes—only to discover that the day-to-day operations of Westcott International generally ran smoothly enough that there was little challenge or excitement in his job. For the first time since he had joined the family business and started his own climb up the corporate ladder, Jordan had realized why his father had so enjoyed buying up various companies in distress and turning them around to show a profit, and why, too, Richard Westcott had engaged in so many daredevil activities—like the hot-air-balloon race that had ended so disastrously, claiming his life.

Just like his father before him, Jordan wanted to make his own mark in the world, not coast along on the long, sturdy coattails of his ambitious, hardworking paternal ancestor who had, in the early nineteenth century, founded what had originally been Westcott Industries, and that, ever since its inception, had been so carefully guarded and nurtured by each successive generation that it had eventually burgeoned into the global enterprise it was today.

Westcott International, based in Chicago, its towering corporate headquarters overlooking Lake Michigan, was currently so huge, diversified and financially solid that it would take a calamity of worldwide proportions to damage it in any significant fashion. Further, Jordan actually had very little to do with many of the companies under its umbrella, keeping tabs on them only through occasional telephone calls and the regular written reports that crossed the expansive antique desk in his penthouse office.

So he was fully aware that the three-month summer vacation he had planned would not adversely affect the family business—and besides, it was not as though he would be unreachable, sequestered in some remote location.

"Darling, you are *not* a figurehead," Sophia declared stoutly, incensed by the very notion—and a little frightened, too, since she had heard the same comment from her late husband on more than one occasion, had seen in his eyes the same adventurous, resolute glint she now spied in their son's. "Westcott International depends on you, as does the family. You're not a child anymore. You're a grown man, and you have serious responsibilities. Surely you are only teasing us about this circus business."

"Mother, I'm not—and if you kept in better touch with Grandpapa, you'd know that." Jordan's tone was now a little stern and accusing, causing Sophia to flush.

"That isn't quite fair, son," she asserted defensively. "You know how your grandpapa is…so proud and stubborn, so determined not to embarrass me or the Westcott family in any way. He wanted so badly for me to make good in life, and now that I have, he doesn't wish to be a reminder of my humble origins— as though I care about that! I've never made a secret of my Gypsy blood or of the fact that I was a circus performer when your father met me and swept me off my feet in a whirlwind courtship.'' Sophia's face softened at the cherished memory, a fond, tender smile curving her lips. ''Richard thought that I was the most exotic, daring woman he'd ever seen. In fact, I think that he was attracted to me precisely because I *was* a trapeze artist and not some tame, well-mannered debutante.''

''But of course, Sophia.'' Chas grinned impudently. ''Every Westcott male in the history of our family has been drawn to women who are wild, beautiful and unique in some way. We have not been known for choosing wives from among the ranks of the reigning queens of society, but, rather, for following the dictates of our hearts. I suppose that being so prudent in business, we must throw caution to the wind elsewhere. Perhaps Jordan has finally succumbed to the Westcott romantic streak, and that's why he has got this crazy idea into his head about your father's circus.''

''Nothing could be further from the truth, Uncle Chas.'' Jordan's thick, unruly black brows were now knitted in a frown of annoyance. ''The Westcott's infamous 'romantic streak,' as you call it, has passed me by. However immodest it may sound, having been the target of many beautiful women—only to discover later on in the relationship that it was my millions that were the real attraction—I'm way too down-to-earth to be bowled over by any gorgeous but wily female these days.''

He grimaced wryly at the thought of his most recently discarded girlfriend, a top model who had eventually revealed to him that she harbored dreams of becoming an actress and had hoped Jordan and his riches would get her into the movies.

"My sole interest is in helping Grandpapa put the Big Top Circus back on a solid financial footing," he continued. "If I were to offer him funds—even in the form of an investment—he would refuse, insisting that I felt sorry for him and was throwing all my hard-earned money away. Mother's right about him being proud and obstinate—besides which, he knows better than anybody how hard it is for a small circus to survive these days. Even the big ones have been forced to merge to stay afloat, there's just so much competition out there for the public's entertainment dollars...concerts, the ballet, touring theater groups, ice shows. The market for circuses simply isn't what it used to be, and the way things stand currently, Grandpapa just can't compete."

"Well, and why should he?" Chas inquired impatiently. "He ought to have sold the Big Top Circus years ago and retired so he could enjoy his remaining years with his family instead of tramping all over the country at his age. I mean, it's not as though we can't take care of him, that he would be a burden. Just the opposite, in fact. He'd be more than welcome."

"Oh, Chas, it's so sweet of you to say that." Sophia patted her brother-in-law's hand affectionately. "But I'm afraid that Jordan's right. The circus is Papa's whole life. Why, his troupe is like a second family to him. He won't willingly give up any of that. Heaven knows, I'm not as out of touch with Papa as

Jordan seems to think. I've tried myself more than once to talk Papa into selling out and coming to live with us. But he won't hear of it. If he only had himself to consider, I think that he might consent. But...well, I believe that he's worried that many of his employees won't be able to find jobs at other circuses. Several members of his troupe have been with him for years. Some are second- and third-generation performers. And as Jordan said, there isn't the market for circuses that there was decades ago."

"Yes, that's true," Charles agreed, nodding soberly. "But, Jordan, you ought to know from all your experience with Westcott International that you can't sell a product there's no market for. So although I certainly admire your good intentions, I'm afraid that I still don't understand how you think that you can help Papa Danior."

"I've already thought of a way," Jordan announced smoothly. "I've informed Grandpapa that my doctor has ordered me to take a leave of absence from my job, that I'm overworked and under way too much stress because of it."

"Well, that's not so very far from the truth, after all." Charles harrumphed and reddened again guiltily. "Come to think of it now, I can't remember the last time you actually had a real vacation, Jordan. You deserve a rest, a little fun in your life for a change. I don't know what Sophia and I were thinking of, trying to prevent you from taking a sabbatical. You're right. Westcott International won't fall apart while you're away, especially if you check in on a regular basis. And my old ticker isn't going to give out if I miss a few golf games. So, what are your plans for the Big Top Circus?''

''I'm going to work for Grandpapa for a while—as a lion tamer.'' Jordan's eyes had begun to dance with mischief, and he grinned wickedly, obviously delighted at the prospect.

''But—but Papa doesn't have any lions in his circus, darling.'' Sophia was clearly bemused.

''He does now. Sixteen lions and lionesses, to be exact. I bought them several weeks ago from a European circus that was closing up shop, and I had them shipped over here to the United States,'' Jordan explained. ''I've got them stashed in one of Westcott International's empty warehouses, and I've been practicing my act on my lunch hour. I'm pretty darned good, even I do say so myself!''

''And just what has Papa had to say about all this?'' Sophia asked, dismayed by this unexpected news. ''Worse, what kind of stories will the media come up with when they find out that the president of an extremely profitable worldwide company is shirking his duties to perform in a second-rate circus? Jordan, they'll... Why, they'll think you've taken leave of your senses! Even your father never did anything *this* wild. This just isn't the sort of thing that's done in business, son. Our shareholders will demand an explanation—and rightly so.''

''Mother, what I choose to do with my own vacation time can be of no interest whatsoever to anyone except myself, and besides, I'm rich enough that I can afford to be more than a little eccentric if I so desire. You know that all the Westcotts are notorious noncomformists, anyway. Only look at the kinds of escapades that Dad used to undertake. Furthermore, I won't be billed as Jordan Westcott. That would be far too dull for the circus. I'm going to be the mysterious Khalif Khan, bold adventurer from the wild African jungles and deserts. And I promise you that I intend to throw myself into the part so thoroughly that no one will ever guess that, in reality, I'm only plain old Jordan Westcott, ho-hum corporate executive.''

"You're anything but ho-hum, darling," Sophia said, not quite sure whether to be glad or exasperated that her son was so hard on himself. "Even so, I can't say that I like this idea at all. Even if you *weren't* president of Westcott International, with all that entails, being a lion tamer is still very dangerous work. Those big cats can turn on you at any moment, Jordan. More than one lion tamer has been badly mauled, even killed in the ring."

"I know that, Mother, and I promise you that I'll take every precaution. But I've just got to do this for Grandpapa. The public thrives on death-defying entertainment, and if he doesn't get some of those types of acts into his circus, he'll wind up being forced to declare bankruptcy and close down entirely or else to sell out to one of his competitors—and either one would break his heart. Besides, once I make myself a part of his circus, I'll be in a much better position to find out how bad things are for him. I can't do that as an outsider, Mother. You know what a closed society the circus is, how protective the performers are of one another, how suspicious they are of those who don't belong. I won't learn anything worthwhile at all if I go in there as Jordan Westcott.''

"Yes, that's true," Sophia acknowledged reluctantly. "I never knew anything about Westcott International until after I'd married your father. He led me to believe that he was a fellow performer, who was down on his luck. I thought he was like that Evel Knievel person, that he did daredevil stunts at local fairs and shows. Why, if I'd known that your father was, in reality, the president of a global enterprise, I wouldn't have had anything to do with him. I'd have felt so inadequate, so awed by his wealth, sophistication and education—"

"Those things just weren't important to Richard, Sophia," Charles observed simply. "He knew that those are things that can be acquired, given the opportunity. It's what's inside a person that's important. Richard saw that you were not only beautiful, but also honest, compassionate and caring—a diamond in the rough, perhaps, but still, a diamond all the same. Those are traits that you've passed on to your son, Sophia. You can't be upset now that they've led him to want to help his grandfather in any way that he can."

"I guess you're right, Chas." Sophia wiped fitfully at the bright tears that had started in her dark eyes. "I'm being selfish, I know. It's just that, well…I've already lost Richard. I don't want to lose Jordan, too."

"You're not going to lose me, Mother." Rising, her son went to sit beside her on the plush chesterfield, putting his strong arms around her and hugging her comfortingly. "No matter what, the risks Dad took were always calculated. He knew what he was doing, and he was always very careful in that regard. I will be, too, I promise."

"I know. But accidents *do* happen, son. Only look at your father!"

"Yes, but, Mother, no one can guard against every single possible mishap. Dad knew that. It's like he always said. One can be crossing the street tomorrow and get run over by a truck. You can't live life worrying all the while that you're going to die. We've got to think about Grandpapa and what's best for him. And if my being a lion tamer will help him, then that's what I must do."

"Of course, you're right, darling." Sophia sighed, forcing herself to put a brave face on the matter.

"He usually is." Chas's tone was rueful at the admission. "Come on, Sophia. I'll cheer you up by taking you out to lunch. Then you can drive the cart while I get in what may be my last eighteen holes the entire summer."

"Oh, Chas, are you sure?" Sophia eyed her brother-in-law a trifle askance, beginning to smile teasingly. "You must remember that the last time I was on a golf course, the cart ran away with me and wound up in that little creek at the thirteenth hole."

"That wasn't your fault," Chas insisted manfully. "The accelerator got stuck. Why, it could have happened to anybody!"

One

At the Big Top
A small city, the Midwest
The present

As she stared at her reflection in the looking glass of the lighted theatrical vanity in her small trailer, Mistral St. Michel sighed heavily. It didn't matter what she did with her cosmetics, she thought dully. She was never going to be a ravishing beauty. She was just too pale and plain, too strangely catlike in appearance, her wide eyes green and slanted, her delicately chiseled nose retroussé, her mouth far too generous for her heart-shaped face. Even her long, silky hair was the tawny color of a lioness's hide. What she was going to do if Nicabar Danior were forced to shut down his circus, she just didn't know.

As a result, Mistral worried endlessly about the future. If she had been stunningly gorgeous, she felt sure that getting a job at another circus might not have seemed to be such an unlikely prospect. But many circuses no longer even had bareback riders, and there was a great deal of competition for trapeze-artist positions, since the more dangerous an act, the more money it tended to earn. So it didn't appear as though either of her specialities would assure her of employment.

She could always work behind the scenes, she supposed glumly, sweeping up or sewing costumes. But that wouldn't be much of a living, or a very secure one, either. And she just *had* to be certain of a decent, stable income. Otherwise, she wouldn't be able to take care of poor old Nicabar, who owned the Big Top Circus and who was the closest thing to family that Mistral had in the entire world.

When she was just a child, her parents, third-generation performers, had been killed in a trapeze accident while working without a net. Since then, because she'd had no other family, Nicabar had raised her, even though she really hadn't been his responsibility at all. For that reason alone, Mistral would have refused to turn her back on him now that he was getting on in years. But the truth was that she couldn't have loved him more if he had been her own grandfather by blood.

So she fretted earnestly whenever she saw the lines

of strain and anxiety on his kindly, weathered face at the small crowds that the Big Top Circus drew, at the sheaf of bills that he shoved into his desk drawer and attempted to make light of, at the ready way he reached into his trouser pocket for a few extra dollars for a fellow performer who needed the money.

Mistral knew that despite how Nicabar tried to protect her, things were a lot worse financially than he let on. And although it was not in her nature to pry, when she had gone to his trailer yesterday morning for their usual small breakfast together, she had spied an unnerving business letter on his desk, her attention attracted by the lavish logo emblazoned across the top of the crisp white bond page. Written by the president of a large, successful circus notorious for squeezing its competition however possible, the missive had clearly been the latest in a series of previous communiqués proposing to buy out the Big Top.

Concerned, Mistral had been unable to prevent herself from hurriedly reading the letter while Nicabar's back was turned. She had been shocked and distressed to realize that far from tendering a friendly offer, the letter had mentioned a buy-out price much less than what was fair for today's market and, further, had been full of snide observations concerning the Big Top's current financial situation and thinly veiled threats about all the difficulties that could befall a small, struggling circus.

When, frightened, Mistral had dared to confront Nicabar about the letter, he had hastily snatched it up and crammed it into his cluttered desk drawer, mumbling that it was nothing, just nonsense penned by a blowhard.

"That's not true, Grandpapa—and deep down inside, you know it!" Mistral had insisted indignantly. "Bruno Grivaldi is an unscrupulous crook, infamous for his strong-arm tactics. Everybody in this business knows that's how his Jungle King Circus got so big in the first place. He has no conscience whatsoever and does whatever it takes to crush his competition— even if it's illegal. Oh, Grandpapa, we have to call the local police and report this."

"Report what?" Nicabar had inquired, shaking his gray-haired head and smiling gently at her fury on his behalf. "That Mr. Grivaldi has made me an offer for the Big Top Circus?"

"No, Grandpapa, of course not. That he has...has *threatened* you!"

"My dearest Mistral...in what way? Does Mr. Grivaldi say in the letter that he is going to kill me? To beat me up? To set fire to my trailer? No...no, he does not. He is far too clever for that. He merely observes that many things may go wrong for a small, struggling circus—and what, I ask you, is so very menacing about that? It is, in fact, true, is it not?"

"Yes, but, Grandpapa, you *know* that he meant it as a threat...a warning that if you don't sell out to him, he intends to make a great deal of trouble for us!" Mistral had declared.

"Maybe." Nicabar had shrugged. "But maybe not. It is not for me to know what goes on inside of Mr. Grivaldi's thick skull. Because no matter what anybody says, I don't think that he can be so very smart, after all. Otherwise, he wouldn't have any interest in my poor little circus. He already has many far bigger acts in his own."

"But not better! There are no finer performers in the business than those in the Big Top! Even Mr. Grivaldi must think so, or surely, he wouldn't bother with us—except that he's just plain greedy and mean, like people say. Grandpapa, you've got to listen to me and file a report with the police!"

"I'm telling you that it won't do any good, Mistral. There's nothing that the authorities can do unless Mr. Grivaldi actually commits some sort of crime against us." Then, seeing the anxiety on the face of the young woman whom he thought of as his granddaughter, Nicabar had spoken more firmly. "But this, we will do, Mistral. I will call the troupe together later on today and warn them that we must be on guard against anything that Mr. Grivaldi might attempt against us. With all of us keeping watch, it will be difficult for Mr. Grivaldi to do us any kind of mischief. Will that help to ease your mind, my dear?"

"I suppose so, Grandpapa... Yes, it's better than nothing, since you won't go to the police." Mistral had sighed, inwardly cursing the affable old man's stubbornness. Nicabar always made up his own mind—and once he had, there was no telling him anything to the contrary. He seldom thought ill of anyone. Mistral had known that he wouldn't truly perceive Bruno Grivaldi as a threat unless he spied his unprincipled rival setting fire to the trailers of the Big Top.

Even worse, however, than Nicabar's refusal to contact the authorities had been the wholly unexpected announcement that had followed.

"Besides," Nicabar had continued, "Mr. Grivaldi isn't going to find the Big Top so easy a target now that I've signed such a wonderful new act for the circus."

"What?" Mistral had exclaimed, startled by this news. Then her eyes had narrowed suspiciously. "What new act, Grandpapa? We are barely scraping by as it is. How can we possibly afford to hire anyone else?"

"Don't you worry about that, my dear. It's all been arranged. Khalif Khan and his lion-tamer act are going to increase our revenues considerably."

"My God, Grandpapa, have you lost your mind? We don't have the cash or credit to buy even the cages, much less a ringful of big cats to go in them! And even if we did, do you know how much it costs to feed and care for lions? And just who is this...this Khalif Khan, anyway? I've never even heard of him! Oh, Grandpapa, whatever were you thinking of? Please tell me that you haven't gone and done anything foolish, that you haven't signed a contract with this man, that you haven't put us even further in debt by purchasing animals that we can't even begin to afford!"

"Now, now, Mistral," Nicabar had said more sternly than was his wont. "I assure you, you're upsetting yourself over nothing. I may be getting on in years, but I'm not senile—at least, not yet, anyway. Khalif Khan is from…Europe. That's why you've never heard of him. He was part of a circus there that got bought out by a larger competitor. They already had a lion tamer and didn't need him. So he wired me about coming here to the United States and joining the Big Top. I've…known him since he was a child, Mistral. I could not turn him down. However, you must not think that Khalif seeks to take advantage of my friendship. He has worked very hard over the years and made some wise investments that paid off for him. As a result, he owns the lions and lionesses that he's bringing with him, and he's agreed to be responsible for their feeding and care. In return, he's to receive a percentage of the gate in addition to his salary. I think that's more than fair, Mistral.''

"But, Grandpapa, if he doesn't help us draw larger crowds, his share of the gate won't amount to enough that those big cats won't go hungry. Then they'll be mean and dangerous.''

"Khalif understands that risk. No, Mistral, I'll hear no further arguments about this. The matter has been settled. You must trust me. You must trust Khalif.''

Trust Khalif, Mistral thought now angrily as she glowered at her reflection in the mirror. Why, she'd sooner trust a snake! She just knew that somehow, some way, this Khalif Khan person had bamboozled her poor old grandfather terribly—no matter if Nicabar believed otherwise. Then another thought struck her—what if the new lion tamer was a plant who worked for Bruno Grivaldi and intended on doing whatever harm he could to the Big Top! It made sense. Why else would he have wanted to join such a small, struggling circus?

Well, he would soon learn his mistake! Mistral told herself hotly. She meant to keep an extremely close watch on this so-called Khalif Khan. If he so much as stepped one toe out of line, she was going to make sure that he was very sorry indeed!

Two

Lions, Tigers and Bears

Hearing a commotion outside in the parking lot of the arena where the Big Top Circus was to perform tomorrow afternoon, Mistral abruptly jumped up from her vanity and ran to her trailer door, flinging it open wide. She would not have been surprised to find that Mr. Grivaldi's henchmen had arrived, that they were even now in the process of doing some irreparable mischief to the Big Top, and she intended to fight tooth and nail if need be to defend the circus.

But instead of the melee that she had expected to see, she spied a huge sixteen-wheeler pulling slowly to a halt in the parking lot. Flamboyantly emblazoned in bright colors upon the sides of the truck's white trailer was an ornate crest with a roaring lion in its center medallion. Printed beneath were the words Big Top Circus, and then, in slightly smaller letters below that, The Incomparable Khalif Khan, Lion Tamer Extraordinaire.

Mistral could hardly believe her eyes. It was not just the dimensions of the sixteen-wheeler, the fact that it looked brand-new, or the flashiness of its paint job that astounded her—although that combination alone was unheard of for a circus the size of the Big Top. No, what actually halted her dead in her tracks was the sight of the vehicle's driver as, after killing the engine, he opened the truck's door and swung down from the cab.

In another time and place, the man would have passed for some marauding desert prince, an Arabian sheikh accustomed to taking what he wanted, Mistral thought in some dim corner of her mind when she saw him. He was at least six feet three inches tall, she judged, with a body to rival the lions that he tamed—powerful, hard, lean and supple. Even his long, shaggy black hair resembled the mane of a big cat, sweeping back from his strongly chiseled, high-boned face to reveal obsidian eyes set beneath thick, swooping brows, and an aquiline nose above a bold, sensual mouth with flashing white teeth.

He moved like one of his lions, too, gracefully but forcefully, so that she could almost feel the tension coiled within him. Beneath the plain white T-shirt that he wore, his muscles bunched and rippled in a way that did something funny to Mistral's insides as she watched him, something that she had never felt before—as though the warm molasses she regularly poured on her pancakes at breakfast were seeping through her entire body, heating her up.

Her gaze traveled down the man's figure, taking in the tight blue jeans that hugged his narrow waist and hips, his corded thighs and calves. Whatever else he might be, Khalif Khan was at least accustomed to hard work, she recognized. There wasn't an ounce of fat on him, just long bones and solid muscle. He looked as though he could hold his own against any of his big cats—and would himself, in fact, be an equally dangerous adversary.

Mistral's eyes narrowed at the notion as she recalled her earlier suspicions that the new lion tamer was, in reality, employed by Bruno Grivaldi and meant to do the Big Top whatever damage he could. Stepping down from her trailer, she made her way determinedly toward the sixteen-wheeler, where her grandfather was now greeting Khalif Khan as though they were indeed the old friends that Nicabar had earlier claimed.

Laughing and calling out to each other, the two men exchanged bear hugs, clapping each other enthusiastically on the back. As she drew near, Mistral observed that there were tears of happiness and deep affection in Nicabar's eyes, and her heart lurched a little with panic at the sight, for until this moment, she had thought that she alone basked in his adoration. Now, she realized with a start that the new lion tamer represented a threat to her in more ways than one.

"Ah, Mistral. There you are, my dear. Come, come," Nicabar urged, smiling and waving her forward, seeming not to notice the anxiety and distrust in her eyes, the scowl on her piquant face. "I want you to meet…Khalif—a very old and dear…friend. In fact, he is like a grandson to me." The old man's black eyes twinkled as he glanced at Jordan, both men delighting in the secret that they shared about the true identity of "Khalif Khan."

"Really?" Mistral snapped, making no attempt to conceal her scorn and disbelief. "In that case, it would've been nice if he'd bothered to keep in touch with you over the years, Grandpapa. Even the occasional postcard from Europe would've sufficed to let you know that he hadn't forgotten you, that he wasn't just some fair-weather friend!"

Her words and attitude made clear to Jordan exactly what she thought of him.

"Actually there've been some improvements over the postal system in this century…such as the telephone, the fax and e-mail," he stated coolly, his broad grin vanishing as he stared at the young woman who stood glaring at him as though he were a stinking pile of elephant dung, needing to be swept up and dumped into a garbage bin.

Just who in the hell did she think she was? he wondered, both angered by and curious about her. He didn't even know her, yet she had not only made no attempt whatsoever to be polite, but she had, in fact, rudely dressed him down. It was something of a novel experience for Jordan. He was not used to being treated like that by a female. Normally they fawned all over him, terribly conscious of his position as president of Westcott International, of the wealth and power that he wielded on a global basis.

Now, the young woman grabbed Nicabar's arm proprietarily and defensively, as though she feared that Jordan intended to harm the old man in some fashion or else to snatch him away from her. Nicabar, however, only continued to smile and patted her hand soothingly.

"Khalif, this is my granddaughter, Mistral," he announced blithely. "I'm afraid that you'll have to forgive her lack of manners. She's not normally so discourteous. But...well, to tell you the truth, things haven't been going as smoothly as they might for the Big Top lately, and that's been most upsetting to Mistral. She's very protective of me."

"Yeah, so I see." Jordan's gaze raked Mistral in a way that made her shiver—not just with uneasiness, but also with some other, indefinable emotion that made her mouth go suddenly dry and her heart begin to pound alarmingly in her breast.

Still, never having been one to run away from her fears, she resolutely stood her ground, lifting her chin defiantly, her green eyes shooting sparks, so that without warning, an image of her naked, bedecked in nothing but the Westcott emeralds locked up in his safe at home, flashed into Jordan's mind. She was, he realized abruptly, beautiful in a strange, wild way that had nothing whatsoever to do with prevailing fashions or magazine covers. Rather, with her long, tawny-gold hair, her wide, slanted, green eyes and her heart-shaped face, she resembled one of the lionesses that he had locked up in the cages inside the sixteen-wheeler—a lioness who badly needed taming.

A wholly unexpected thrill coursed through Jordan at the idea. Of course, this young woman knew absolutely nothing about him, his money, or Westcott International. She believed that he was Khalif Khan, lion tamer extraordinaire. What an opportunity!

Much to Mistral's puzzlement and suspicion, as she looked at him, a mocking smile suddenly curved Khalif's bold, sensual mouth, and his black eyes glittered in a manner that sent another peculiar shudder stabbing through her.

Her first impression of him had been right, she thought nervously. He was definitely not a man to cross, a man who would back away from a challenge. He was rather, a lethal predator just like his lions. Instead of dampening any unsavory expectations or plans he might have, her combative attitude had clearly aroused his own contentious instincts.

Silently, biting her lower lip, Mistral cursed her stupidity soundly. She had accomplished nothing but to provoke Khalif's unwelcome interest and put him on his guard. What a fool she was! If he were indeed, as she suspected, one of Bruno Grivaldi's hirelings, he would now be wary of her. Or worse! For the way the lion tamer was staring at her, she felt as though she were standing there without any clothes on, that he knew exactly what she looked like stark naked! Still grinning, as though aware of her indignation and discomfiture, Khalif now actually had the audacity to abruptly stick out his hand.

"Pleased to meet you, Mistral," Jordan drawled impudently. "All these years, hearing about Nicabar's granddaughter, I had in mind a little girl, some sad-eyed orphan. It hadn't occurred to me until just this moment that you'd be all grown up by now, a self-possessed young woman."

It was as though, instead of offering to shake her hand, Khalif had tossed down a gauntlet between them, Mistral reflected heatedly. Her palm itched almost uncontrollably to slap that self-assured smirk right off his swarthy, handsome face. Instead, gritting her teeth, she forced herself to shake hands with him, totally unprepared for the shocking tremor that jolted through her at the contact of their flesh. If she hadn't known better, she would have suspected him of concealing a clown's electric buzzer in his palm. Her breath caught in her throat, and she would have jerked her hand away rudely had he not grasped it so tightly, yet with a curious gentleness that surprised and dismayed her.

What in the blazes was the matter with her? Mistral asked herself furiously. This man might be here to sabotage the Big Top—and instead of knocking the wind from his sails, she was standing here like a complete idiot, her emotions in an utterly untypical and bewildering turmoil.

Try as she might, Mistral was unable to free her

hand from his own. Her palm felt as though it had
ignited at his touch, that flames were now licking up
her arm, burning their way through her entire body.
A hot tide of crimson color flooded her cheeks at the
sudden, startling realization that despite everything,
she was physically attracted to the lion tamer.

Good Lord! What was she thinking of? The very
idea was ridiculous! Khalif Khan had unnerved her,
that was all—the same way that a fall from the trapeze or the bare back of one of her horses did. In a
moment, she would get her bearings and her breath,
Mistral told herself firmly—and at last she did, insistently withdrawing her hand from his.

"I trust that Grandpapa's already informed you
about how the Big Top runs, Mr. Khan," she said,
her tone low and clipped. "But just in case he hasn't,
you should know that I handle the management of the
actual circus operations, while Grandpapa takes care
of all the finances, bookings and so forth."

"Yeah, he's explained all that." Jordan's mouth
still twitched with humor. Dressed in a Versace suit
and armed with a leather portfolio, Mistral St. Michel
would have been right at home in a corporate boardroom, he mused.

He'd be willing to wager his last dollar that whatever problems the circus had, he wasn't going to find
out that they stemmed from mismanagement of its
day-to-day operations. He'd bet this gorgeous lioness
ran everything as smoothly and tightly as was possible under the circumstances—that nobody was ped-
dling fifty-pound sacks of horse feed out from under

her delicate, turned-up nose or bedecking their costumes with forty-dollars-a-bag glass beads.

So although, much to his bemusement, Mistral was decidedly wreaking havoc on his senses physically, Jordan was greatly relieved mentally to discover that Nicabar's adopted granddaughter wasn't likely to be robbing the generous old man blind or running the Big Top financially into the ground through sheer stupidity and gross incompetence. In fact, from what he had seen thus far, she appeared to be as genuinely fond of his grandfather as Jordan himself was, as sincerely devoted to protecting and helping Nicabar.

For an instant, Jordan was strongly tempted to take her into his confidence. But then, reluctantly, he decided against it. In reality, he knew next to nothing about Mistral St. Michel. Indeed, until this moment, he had actually quite forgotten her very existence. She couldn't have been much more than a toddler during his childhood and teens, when he had spent his summers with his grandfather at the Big Top, learning all about the circus, from the ground up. There was hardly anything that Jordan hadn't tried his hand at over the years—which was why he knew all about lion taming to begin with.

Twenty years ago, the Big Top hadn't been so small and struggling. Back then, it had boasted not only lions, but also tigers, bears and even elephants. Jordan had worked with all those animals at one time or another; and although it had been a while since those halcyon days of his youth, it was just like riding a bicycle: Once you learned how, you never forgot.

He had been shaky at first in the lion ring, but he had quickly regained his footing and confidence during his practice sessions at the Westcott International warehouse, where he had stashed the big cats that he had acquired from the European circus that had gone under.

"So, Mistral, where would you like me to unload?" Jordan queried, letting her know with the casual question that he accepted her management of the circus and didn't intend to offer any challenge to her authority—at least, not unless he had totally misread her.

She motioned around the largely empty parking lot of the arena where the Big Top was to give its matinee performance tomorrow. "Wherever is convenient for you, Mr. Khan." Mistral now spoke with exaggerated politeness, putting him on notice that she was certain that he was a troublemaker and that he had in no way fooled her with his deference. She would have liked to say more. But after a moment, she thought better of it, and biting her tongue to hold back the scathing words that had sprung to it, she abruptly pivoted and strode back to her trailer, leaving Jordan alone with his grandfather.

"Pay her no mind," Nicabar told his grandson amiably, inwardly amused and pleased by the sparks that he had felt emanating between the two young people. "She worries about me and the Big Top. She's afraid that we can't afford you and your big cats, Jordan. Even worse, I think that she suspects that you've been sent here by Bruno Grivaldi."

"Bruno Grivaldi, Grandpapa?" Jordan had heard the name before.

"The man who owns the Jungle King Circus. He's made more than one offer to buy out the Big Top, but of course, I've refused to sell. In addition to being a greedy, hard-nosed businessman intent on crushing or swallowing all his competition, Mr. Grivaldi has few, if any, scruples, I fear. Mistral believes that he means to do us some harm. That's one of the reasons why I agreed to your plan to join the Big Top for the summer, Jordan. I know that you have much better ways to spend your well-deserved vacation, that you're doing this to help me out financially—no matter how much you may deny it. Under ordinary circumstances, I would be upset by this, you understand. But frankly, I'm worried that Mistral may be right about Mr. Grivaldi. The last small circus that refused to sell out to him was mysteriously burned to the ground one night. For myself, I do not mind taking such a risk. But for Mistral and the rest of my troupe, and for my animals, I have grave concerns—such that I would have accepted Mr. Grivaldi's offer had I not known in my heart that he would turn most of my performers and beasts out to starve."

"Grandpapa! Why didn't you tell me all this before?" Jordan inquired, frowning.

"I didn't want you and Sophia fretting about me. I may be getting on in years, but I still know how to take care of myself. And you know how your mother is. Why, she would have hired a private security force at the very least to guard me and the Big Top! We couldn't have borne that, Jordan. It would have been too humiliating. We circus people look after our own. We always have, and as long as there are still circuses, we always will. That's why I took Mistral in after her parents were killed. That's why she worries about me and the Big Top, and why you mustn't be put off by that rather large chip on her shoulder. She has far too many heavy responsibilities for such a young woman, I'm afraid. She ought to be out enjoying life instead of looking after an old man and his dream. I'll feel much better about her safety and well-being now that you're here.''

"I won't let anything happen to her—or the circus—I promise, Grandpapa.'' Jordan was wholly outraged at the notion of Bruno Grivaldi thinking that he could intimidate Nicabar into selling the Big Top, that the unscrupulous proprietor of the Jungle King Circus might actually attempt to harm Nicabar, Mistral and the Big Top.

Although despite his reassurances to the contrary to his mother and uncle, Jordan had secretly half feared that his plan to spend the summer with his grandfather's circus had been a wild idea at best, he was now glad that he had hit upon the scheme. In checking around for the lions and cages that he had bought, he had heard more than one ugly rumor about Mr. Grivaldi.

Fortunately Jordan knew the type. If Mr. Grivaldi or his henchmen came nosing around to cause trouble at the Big Top, Jordan would know how to deal with them!

Three

A Ringside Seat

Returning to her trailer, Mistral banged the door shut behind her and locked it. She had never felt as confused in her life as she did right now. She was both angry and ashamed. She had marched out there to the parking lot and made a complete fool of herself—hadn't even given Khalif Khan a chance before passing judgment on him and speaking to him as though he were a thief whom she had caught pilfering supplies from the circus! She just didn't know what had got into her—except that her worries about the Big Top and Bruno Grivaldi had driven her to see shadows in every corner.

But what if she were wrong? What if she had made a dreadful mistake, and Khalif *didn't* work for Mr. Grivaldi? She would have treated the lion tamer abominably for no good reason whatsoever, possibly even making an enemy of a man who might actually be of some assistance to the Big Top. That just wasn't like her at all. She had completely lost her head, given free rein to her quick, hot temper—the bane of her existence. Many times, Mistral had attempted to restrain it, to force herself to calm down and count to ten before giving vent to her turbulent emotions. Normally she succeeded. But today, she hadn't.

Somehow, it was all that blasted lion tamer's fault! she concluded irrationally. There was just something about him that had affected her like a conk on the head, leaving her dazed and reeling. Moving to one of the trailer windows, she furtively drew back the lacy curtain a little to peek out into the parking lot. Aided by various of the Big Top's male employees, Khalif was unloading from the sixteen-wheeler the cages containing the lions.

Well, at least that was a mark in his favor, Mistral thought—that he didn't plan on keeping the animals shut up constantly in the truck's trailer or even in the arena's large, underground area, where they wouldn't get any fresh air or sunlight.

Through the screens of her trailer's open windows, she could hear him talking to the big cats, calling each one by name, affectionately teasing some, speaking soothingly to others made anxious by all the racket and the strangers milling around. More than once,

Khalif stuck his hand between the iron bars of the cages to scratch the head and ears of one of the lionesses, who comprised the majority of the big cats.

In the wild, the females were generally both the hunters and nurturers, doing all the work, while the lazy males were the first in line to gorge themselves on the prey brought down by the lionesses. The males sometimes killed the pride's cubs, too, so that the lionesses would come into season again, ready to be mated.

For this reason, Mistral didn't think much of lions. They reminded her of many of the men whom she had known over the years in the circus—men who regularly drank up their paychecks and then abused their wives and children. She knew that circus life was hard. But still, that was no excuse.

Idly she wondered if Khalif were married. She didn't think so. Had that been the case, Nicabar would surely have said something about it—besides which, Khalif himself had arrived alone. Of course, it was possible that he had a wife and kids stashed over in Europe, that he simply hadn't brought them with him to the United States. Still, that seemed unlikely.

"Not that it should make any difference whatsoever to you one way or the other, Mistral, my girl," she muttered to herself, annoyed. "What do you care if the man is married or not?"

She didn't, she reassured herself fiercely. She didn't want or need a man in her life, messing up her trailer, her finances, her dreams and possibly even her face. Nicabar was right. She needed to concentrate on her studies so that she could better her lot in life.

The employable years for a circus performer were short, and Mistral knew that hers were numbered. How much longer could she realistically hope to go on bouncing along on the bare back of one of her horses or flying through the air on the trapeze? Sooner or later, if her career wasn't ended by a serious injury, sheer age alone would catch up with her.

Of course, she could continue on like Nicabar, as a ringleader and in a management capacity. But at this point, the prospect that she would one day be running the Big Top by herself didn't look very good. The small circus was barely able to stave off its creditors. One costly mishap would prove a deathblow to it financially.

Besides which, Mistral knew that Nicabar had actual blood relatives somewhere, a daughter and a grandson who might not be very keen on the idea of her taking over the Big Top. If and when Nicabar ever decided finally to retire, his relatives might be disposed to selling the circus instead.

For that reason, whenever she could, Mistral pored over books, reading whatever she could lay her hands on to further the haphazard tutoring that she had received as a child traveling with the circus. As a result, despite that she had only a GED, she actually had a far better and broader education than many people with college degrees.

Under Nicabar's tutelage, she was currently learning how to handle much of the business side of the circus. With a few more years under her belt, she felt that she would have good management skills, that if she were compelled to give up the Big Top at the end of her performing career, she would have other marketable assets.

But that time was not now and a husband—a fellow circus performer—was definitely not on her list of items to acquire for a secure future. She could take care of herself. Still, despite herself, Mistral continued to peek out the window at Khalif.

It just wasn't right, she thought crossly, for any male to be so damned attractive. It was bad enough that he was without a doubt the most handsome man whom she had ever laid eyes on. Far worse was the compelling animal magnetism that had seemed to emanate from him in waves, that had made her feel as though she were on fire when he had taken her hand in his.

Slowly Mistral glanced down at her palm, as though expecting to discover that it had been seared to a crisp by Khalif's touch. To her surprise, it didn't look any different from before. Involuntarily she pressed it to her lips, half expecting to find that it was still warm and pulsing. But it was now as cool as the refreshing summer breeze that gently billowed the lacy curtains at the windows of her trailer inward.

Still, she remembered the feel of Khalif's heated flesh against hers. His hand had been well-shaped, long and elegant, yet surprisingly strong and curiously gentle. And smooth. Mistral's brow knitted in a puzzled frown at that realization, her eyes narrowing once more with suspicion, her nape beginning to tingle. His hand had been *smooth,* the nails well kept and clean.

Circus performers didn't have hands like that.

Her own palms were rough and callused—from resin and the trapeze bar, from helping to erect the safety net and from mucking out the trailers of her horses...countless things that were part and parcel of being a circus performer, of lending a hand wherever it was needed in a small operation like the Big Top, where everybody pitched in and no chore was beneath a performer's dignity. She clenched her fists abruptly.

Khalif Khan didn't have circus hands...or even hands that looked as though they did any kind of regular manual labor whatsoever. But how was that possible? Mistral asked herself slowly, stunned. It could mean only two things: Either Nicabar had been duped by Khalif, or else he had deliberately lied to her about him. She just wouldn't, *couldn't* believe the latter explanation. Her grandfather might hide bills from her to prevent her from fretting, but he would never purposefully conceal something important from her—at least, not without an excellent cause.

That left the former explanation, that her grandfather had been fooled, badly taken in by the lion tamer. Khalif Khan. What kind of a name was that, anyway? Mistral now wondered hotly. Not a real one, surely, but, rather, a name chosen for its theatrical flair.

Because the Big Top was such a small circus, all of its performers had at least two or three different stage names. The bareback riders—who doubled as the trapeze act—were known as the Galloping Gitanas when they appeared with their horses. When they were flying through the air above their safety net, they were billed as the Spectacular Solanas.

Mistral had always believed that the public was smart enough to figure out that nobody in either act was actually related and, further, that most of the performers did double duty. Even so, she invariably wore her hair down as a Gitana and up as a Solana, feeling that its unusual tawny color would otherwise be noticed by the crowd and spoil the illusion every circus hoped to create—of mysterious, exotic performers and magical, fantastical feats of daring.

But it would be difficult for a man like Khalif Khan to engage in those chameleonlike tactics. He was too physically striking, taller by far than most circus performers, who tended as a whole to be much smaller and more compact than he was. No matter what, he would always stand out in a crowd—which made it all that much more unlikely that Mistral had never heard of him. Surely his presence was such that had he been a performer all his life, he would now be as well-known as Gunther Goebbels or Siegfried and Roy or half a dozen others whom she could name.

"Oh, that Khalif Khan must be a complete and utter sham!" Mistral told herself now, her blood boiling again. "Why, he must, in reality, be an—an arsonist or something—maybe even a—a *hit man!* That horrible Bruno Grivaldi must have hired him to burn down the Big Top—or perhaps even to kill Grandpapa!"

Such was her fear and rage at this last that she

almost marched outside to confront the lion tamer once more, to tell him that he was fired and that she wanted him off the premises immediately. But then it dawned on her that Nicabar almost certainly would not back her up in such a decision, and, worse, that even if he did, the result would be that Khalif Khan would leave the circus and then she would have no way of knowing what treachery Mr. Grivaldi was scheming.

No, she reasoned, trying to curb her temper. It was better to remain silent and on her guard. That way, she could perhaps learn how Mr. Grivaldi intended to strike out at the Big Top.

He had already proved himself inordinately clever. To do his dirty work, he had employed someone whom he must have discovered that her grandfather had known for years and trusted. That was the only logical explanation for why poor old Nicabar had been so totally deceived.

How very hurt and upset he was going to be when he found out the truth! Mistral's heart ached for him. Her grandfather had always been too honest and trusting for his own good, never wanting to think ill of anyone. That was why she was so protective of him.

With a terse imprecation, she allowed the lacy curtain to drop back into place, forcing herself to turn away from the window. Of course, it was only natural that she should have been attracted to the lion tamer. She had little real experience with men—and certainly none at all with anyone like him. He was handsome and magnetic enough to have turned any woman's head, including that of one much more worldly than Mistral.

But now that she knew Khalif Khan for the fraud that he was, she would not be so easily drawn. She would keep a close, intensely watchful eye on him— and instruct the others in the troupe to do the same. Sooner or later, they would surely catch the lion tamer in some malicious, heinous act, and then her grandfather would be compelled to contact the police— whether he wished to or not!

Beginning to tidy up her trailer in a sudden burst of energy borne of her fury, Mistral took great delight in imagining Khalif Khan locked up in a cage somewhere—just like his lions.

Four

Popcorn, Peanuts, Cotton Candy

It had long been Mistral's custom to cook dinner for her grandfather every evening, just as he prepared breakfast for the two of them each morning, and tonight was no different—except that much to her dismay, when Nicabar appeared at her trailer door, he had Khalif Khan in tow.

"I hope that you don't mind, my dear, but I've invited Khalif to join us. It seemed the only courteous thing to do, since he has no family here and he hasn't had much of an opportunity to make any real friends at the Big Top. If not for my invitation, he would have dined alone, and that surely wouldn't have been right, especially on his first night as part of our circus family,'' Nicabar explained.

Other than to rudely eject the lion tamer from the steps of her trailer, Mistral didn't know what she could do prevent him from coming in, and silently, she cursed her grandfather for not seeking her permission prior to issuing the invitation to supper—not that she had ever minded Nicabar's generosity before. He was always asking people to eat with them, and she had never raised any objections, as happy as he to share their evening meal with fellow performers.

"If my being here is an imposition, I can always grab a bite somewhere else." Jordan had noticed that Mistral was not exactly enthusiastic about having him as a dinner guest. To his surprise, he discovered that he was unhappy with the idea that she had clearly made up her mind to dislike him, thinking that he was taking advantage of Nicabar.

"It's no trouble at all to set another plate," Mistral insisted, forcing herself to smile welcomingly, reminding herself that the only way that she was going to learn what Khalif was up to was to lull him into a false sense of security. She couldn't do that if she tossed him out on his ear the very first thing. "Won't you please come in?" She opened the door for the two men.

They stepped inside, and immediately, it seemed to Mistral that her trailer—not large to begin with—shrank several feet in size and increased several degrees in temperature. Even Otto Wetzler, the circus's strong man, did not dominate his surroundings the way that the lion tamer did. She had an unbidden mental impression that compared Khalif in her trailer to one of his lions in its cage, both of them taking up space, prowling and straining at their confines.

"Please...sit down." Mistral motioned toward the built-in dining booth, where she had already laid two place settings. "I'll just get another plate and take supper off the stove." As she busied herself in the small kitchen, she surreptitiously studied Khalif.

His appearance hadn't changed in the interval between this afternoon and this evening, so that she knew her eyes hadn't been deceiving her earlier. He was without a doubt the most handsome man whom she had ever seen. Despite herself, just looking at him made her mouth water.

Mistral swallowed hard, fuming at herself for being such a fool. Why, she might have been some silly, smitten schoolgirl instead of a grown woman! She didn't like the sense that she had lost control of her reason and emotions. She needed to get hold of herself. Otherwise, she wasn't going to be of any help to Nicabar whatsoever by finding out how Khalif and his probably real boss Mr. Grivaldi planned to sabotage the Big Top.

With that thought in mind, Mistral forced herself to concentrate on getting the food on the table. She could have kicked herself for not realizing that Nicabar would almost surely invite the lion tamer to dinner. If she had given the matter any consideration at all, she would have known that this would indeed prove to be the case, and she would have prepared something much more elaborate than just the simple meal that she had cooked—a hearty beef stew, a Caesar salad and hot, crusty French bread.

But why should it make any difference what she had fixed? she asked herself irritably. She didn't care what Khalif thought. If he weren't impressed with her culinary skills, he could go chow down a fat burger at some greasy spoon. It certainly wasn't her goal in life to impress the new lion tamer.

Grabbing pot holders from a drawer, Mistral lifted the pot of stew off the stove, emptying it into an attractive, hand-painted tureen that she had picked up somewhere during the circus's travels over the years. Normally she would have just served both herself and her grandfather—and even their fellow performers— right off the stove, so that there wouldn't be as many dishes to wash later. But, inexplicably, there was something about Khalif that urged her to adopt a more formal approach. She didn't know what.

Other than the fact that he was drop-dead gorgeous and had the hands of a man who didn't do manual labor for a living, he was really no different from any of the other male performers in the circus. As they would have been, he was still dressed simply, now in a pale blue chambray work shirt, blue jeans and a pair of black boots. It was just that, given the different shirt, he had unquestionably changed clothes before coming to her trailer.

His attire was pristine clean—not dirty, stained with sweat, grease, or manure, as it would have been had he worn it all day long—and it appeared somehow...expensive, too, Mistral thought. On him, the shirt looked as though it had stepped right out of the pages of a fancy catalog or something, and his jeans had actually been starched and pressed. She could see the razor crease in them that proclaimed that astonishing fact. The boots that he wore had been polished until they shone like new, and they were fashioned of some jazzy reptilian leather. They didn't have scuffed toes or run-down heels, either.

Obviously Nicabar hadn't lied when he'd told her that Khalif had made some smart investments over the years—or else it was simply that Mr. Grivaldi was paying the lion tamer a real tidy sum to do his dirty work for him.

Taking the salad from the refrigerator, Mistral covertly dumped it from its plastic container into a decorative ceramic bowl that matched the tureen. Then she added a pair of salad tongs—wishing that they were sterling silver instead of plastic. The French bread went onto a breadboard, and before carrying it to the table, she cut a few slices, the same way that she had seen it displayed in the magazines that she read about homes, gardens and cooking. She poured the tea that she had brewed earlier into a glass pitcher and tossed in ice and lemons.

"Well, I guess that's everything," she said, joining the men at the table.

"It smells wonderful," Jordan declared as she lifted the lid on the tureen and the savory aroma of the stew wafted to his nostrils.

Indeed, despite the fact that Mistral clearly shopped

at discount stores and flea markets, he had found himself impressed by her trailer and the table. He knew that because it was a vagabond way of life filled with animals and manual labor, many people associated circuses with untidiness and dirt.

But there was nothing disorderly or unclean about Mistral's trailer. It was simply but attractively furnished and as neat as the proverbial pin, lacking the clutter and disarray of many performers' trailers. She had covered the table with a red-checkered cloth that hung down nearly to the floor. Over it, she had laid a matching, multicolored quilt the size of a baby's blanket. A glass vase of mixed flowers sat in the center. The place settings were bright Fiesta ware, the flatware plain stainless steel, the glasses different colored plastic tumblers. There were red-checkered cloth napkins.

It was, of course, nothing to rival the Honduras-mahogany dining table in his penthouse apartment, laden with Limoges china, sterling silverware engraved with the Westcott initial and Baccarat crystal. But it had a quaint, appealing charm that let Jordan know that Mistral had made the most of what she had been able to afford. She had taste, he recognized, and it wasn't garish. Idly he wondered what she might accomplish if she had access to a bank account the size of his.

"If I'd known that you were going to be dining with us, I'd have prepared something more substantial," Mistral explained as she began to ladle the steaming stew into bowls. "But Grandfather and I eat very simply when it's just the two of us." She didn't add that they couldn't afford much, in any event.

"What's here will be just fine." Jordan helped himself to the salad and bread, realizing suddenly that after working so hard physically all day, he was starving in a way that he never was usually.

"Yes, Mistral is an excellent cook," Nicabar bragged, proud of his granddaughter. "And everything looks so festive, my dear. You didn't need to go to so much trouble for us."

Mistral practically bit off her tongue to stifle the censorious words that rose to her lips. As much as she loved him, she felt like kicking her grandfather in the shins under the table. Crimson stained her cheeks. She didn't want Khalif Khan to think that she had done anything special on his account.

"Don't worry, Grandfather. I didn't. I'm just a little tired this evening, so I thought that it would be easier to serve at the table, that's all," she lied.

"Well, it's all very nice, and the stew is delicious." Jordan hadn't failed to notice how agitated Mistral appeared at Nicabar's observations. She was blushing as though she were embarrassed. Either she didn't like a fuss to be made, he thought, or else she was the shy type, unsure how to accept compliments.

"Mr. Khan, I want to apologize to you for my...abruptness this afternoon," Mistral said. "I'm afraid that I didn't welcome you properly to the Big Top. I was just so...surprised by your joining us. I'm sure that Grandpapa has explained to you that we're a small, struggling circus—"

"And you're worried about the financial strain that I and my lions might prove," Jordan interjected smoothly. "But you really needn't be. I handle the care and feeding of my lions myself. I always have. They belong to me and not to any circus. That makes them my responsibility."

"Yes, I understand. However, it may be that you were assured of far larger crowds in Europe, where circuses have long been a popular tradition—although it would seem that the one by which you were previously employed was not immune to the difficulties that currently plague the market. It was the…Sparkles Circus that you were with before, was it not?"

"Spangles," Jordan corrected, not revealing by so much as a flicker of his eyelash that he was lying through his teeth and wished that she would find some other line of inquiry.

Still, she was not going to be the only one at the Big Top to exhibit suspicions, to question his background. He only hoped that no one would prove capable of blowing his cover—although he was thinking that a great deal of innate intelligence lurked in Mistral's slanted green eyes. She was not going to be easy to fool.

He had been unforgivably arrogant, he realized abruptly, trusting that his Ivy League education and years of corporate experience would prove more than a match for the performers employed by the Big Top. They might not have had his advantages in life, but that didn't make them stupid.

"It was a circus very much like this one, actually,"

he continued, sticking to the story that he and Nicabar had agreed on between them. "Unfortunately when the owners decided to merge with another, larger circus, I was out of a job. That's when I got in touch with Nicabar, figuring to try my luck here in the United States. I believe that I can help the Big Top, Mistral. Otherwise, I wouldn't be here."

"I'm not doubting your word, Mr. Khan—"

"Khalif. Please, call me Khalif," Jordan urged politely.

"But that's surely not your real name," Mistral said pointedly.

"No. However, I have...used it for so long that any other would seem strange to me."

"All right, then. Khalif it is. As I was saying, I'm not doubting your word, only questioning whether or not you made your decision fully informed of the state of the market here in the United States. It's very difficult for a circus to compete these days for the public's entertainment dollars. I'd just hate to think that you came all the way from Europe—only to find yourself in the same boat as before, that's all."

"All of life is a gamble, Mistral. As the old saying goes, you pays your money, and you takes your chances. I enjoy the work that I do for a living, so I was willing to take a risk in coming here."

"Well, I hope that everything turns out, then. However, I'm sure that Grandpapa must have informed you that the Big Top has been...approached by another, larger circus, as well—the Jungle King. Perhaps you've heard of it?"

"Yeah, even in Europe, the Jungle King Circus was known," Jordan remarked dryly. "There were...several rather unpleasant rumors about its owner, Bruno Grivaldi. It seems that he utilizes some highly questionable tactics in his bids to take over smaller operations."

Based on the information that Nicabar had imparted to him today, Jordan had earlier this evening, via the notebook computer that he'd brought along with him, instructed various members of his staff at Westcott International to investigate the Jungle King Circus and Mr. Grivaldi, to uncover everything that they could find and send it to him as soon as possible.

"Indeed. So I, too, have heard." Mistral's heart was pounding. She had never expected Khalif to admit being familiar with the Jungle King Circus, much less with its unscrupulous owner. He was either very clever or very brazen, she concluded, so sure of himself and his success at overcoming any obstacles in his path that he felt comfortable acknowledging an awareness of the shark who was after the Big Top.

Mistral didn't know anything about criminals other than what she had read in novels and magazines. However, she thought that Khalif must be dangerous indeed to be so cocksure. For a moment, she had an almost uncontrollable urge to dump the tureen of stew in his lap, scalding him so that he would have to be carried away to a hospital. But then she considered his wrath at his release, and she shivered, feeling as though a goose had just walked over her grave.

His eyes were as black as jet. When he looked at

her, it was as though he could see into her very soul....

Stop it, Mistral! Just stop it! she told herself silently, angrily. *You're letting your wild imagination run away with you. For all you really know, the man is exactly what he's claimed. It's just too incredible to believe that he's an arsonist—or, heaven forbid, a hit man. Think about it. Why would Mr. Grivaldi go to so much trouble over the Big Top, anyway, sending in not only a lion tamer, but also a whole parcel of lions to go with him? That just doesn't make any sense. That would cost Mr. Grivaldi an inordinate amount of money. It would be easier for him simply to pay a fair price for the Big Top.*

Deep down inside, Mistral knew that, logically, this was indeed the case. Still, she couldn't seem to overcome her apprehensions.

"After reading Mr. Grivaldi's last letter to the Big Top, I told Grandpapa that we should contact the police and file a report," she announced, to let Khalif know that she would not be slow to call in the authorities should there be any mischief done to the circus. "But Grandpapa felt that at this point, we would be prudent merely to alert the troupe and be on our guard, since Mr. Grivaldi has been shrewd enough to couch his threats in ways that leave them open to interpretation."

"Indeed." Jordan echoed Mistral's earlier word and tone. A frown had now appeared on his face, and he glanced accusingly at Nicabar, knowing from Mistral's dialogue that their grandfather had deliberately made the threat to the Big Top seem less than it really was. "Do you think that was wise, Nicabar, given Mr. Grivaldi's reputation?"

Nicabar shrugged sheepishly, refusing to look Jordan in the eye. "What else could I do? I have no proof that Mr. Grivaldi is anything other than an astute, however hard-nosed, businessman," he insisted. "Despite what Mistral thinks, I would only have looked foolish—a senile old man with a failing circus and seeing shadows in every corner as a result. No, no. It is best for now to handle the matter in the fashion that I have decided. The troupe can keep watch. There are enough of us for that, to observe any strangers who may attempt to finagle their way backstage or who show up to hang around the circus between performances. Otto—that's Otto Wetzler, our strong man—is very big and powerful. He knows how to deal with unwelcome visitors."

"Still, Gr—Nicabar—"

"Please, Khalif, why don't you call me Grandpapa, like you used to in the old days? After so many years of friendship, we are...almost family, you and I, are we not? It will be easier that way, no?"

"Yeah." Jordan nodded, silently cursing his small slip of the tongue. He had tried so hard to be careful, but it was difficult to remember to address his grandfather as Nicabar. "As I was saying...Grandpapa, even if there's nothing specific that you can point to where Mr. Grivaldi is concerned, wouldn't it be better at least to have filed a report?"

"I don't see why." Nicabar shook his head. "Who

is going to take me seriously without any hard evidence? And if and when Mr. Grivaldi decided to move against us, we could be hundreds of miles away from the city where I filled out such a report—if the authorities would even bother to keep it on file.''

"Perhaps you're right," Jordan acknowledged slowly.

Mistral longed to strangle him. At first, when he had seemed to disagree with Nicabar about getting in touch with the authorities, she had thought that she had misjudged Khalif badly. Now, she saw that he was even smarter and slier than she had suspected, leading her grandfather down the proverbial primrose path—only to knife him in the back at some later date, she felt certain.

Under any circumstances, she would have been hurt and, yes, even jealous that Nicabar appeared to be taking Khalif under his wing, just as the old man had assumed responsibility for her so many years ago. But the idea that Nicabar would ask Khalif to call him Grandpapa when the lion tamer surely meant the Big Top no good galled and wounded Mistral no end. It was all that she could do to blink back the hot tears that had stung her eyes at Nicabar's request.

Fortunately, neither man noticed. They had eaten their way enthusiastically through most of the salad, stew and bread, absorbed by the food and their discussion. But now, both the meal and the conversation stuck in Mistral's throat. Mumbling her excuses and rising, she moved to the tiny kitchen to scrape her plate off into the trash can, the sink not boasting a garbage disposal.

"Would either of you like dessert?" she queried, compelling herself to smile brightly. "I know how much you adore apple pie, Grandpapa, so I baked one for you earlier today." Mistral didn't want to admit— even to herself—that she had made the treat in an attempt to bind Nicabar to her, that she felt irrationally as though she were losing him somehow to Khalif Khan.

"I'd love a piece, Mistral." Nicabar grinned back at her fondly, his eyes twinkling. "And if you have some vanilla ice cream to top it off with, I wouldn't say no to that, either."

"You always did have a sweet tooth, Grandpapa," Jordan remarked. "I remember in the old days how you used to personally check to ensure that the cotton-candy machine was working properly."

"You don't think that I'd forget your ice cream, do you, Grandpapa?" Mistral asked as though Khalif had not spoken—although she nevertheless felt guilty and ashamed of herself for interrupting, for competing like a child with the lion tamer for Nicabar's attention. Then, flushing and biting her lower lip as she saw Khalif's eyebrows raise in silent curiosity and rebuke, she turned her attention to slicing the pie and scooping up the ice cream. She made coffee, too, in the coffeemaker on the counter.

To her surprise, while she worked, the lion tamer rose to finish clearing the table for her, bringing the rest of the dishes over to the sink.

"You didn't need to do that," Mistral said tersely, unnerved by his proximity. She was unused to being around men who were so big and tall, and since the kitchen area in her trailer was quite tiny, he seemed to loom over her, filling up the space, so that it was as though if she moved, she would run right into him. That would, she thought, be like colliding with a brick wall, his body was so hard and muscular.

"You cooked, and besides, I've never been the kind of man who objects to cleaning up after a meal," Jordan said. Then, seeing the difficulty that she was having trying to get the ice cream, which was frozen rock solid, out of the container, he continued. "Here. Let me help you with that."

Before Mistral could protest, he had come up behind her, wrapping his hand around hers on the ice-cream scoop. As it had earlier that day, his touch sent an electric thrill coursing through her that left her confused and trembling. She could feel his breath warm against her skin, prickling the fine hairs on her nape. His free hand had snaked around her to close over her own, which held the ice-cream container to keep it from shifting, so that, now, she could feel, too, the muscles that bunched and rippled sensuously in his arm, pressed against her.

"Really, I can do it myself," Mistral insisted, startled and embarrassed by the sound of her voice, unfamiliarly low and husky.

"No, the ice cream's hard." And he was swiftly becoming that way himself, as well, Jordan realized as he guided her hand, digging the scoop into the container.

She smelled as sweet and vanilla as the ice cream, so that he yearned to bury his face against her hair and skin, to feel her tawny tresses sliding like silk through his fingers, the smoothness of her satiny flesh beneath his palms. He wanted her—as he had not wanted a woman in a long while, so jaded and cynical had he grown. The recognition surprised him. Earlier that afternoon, he had been alternately attracted to, bemused and annoyed by her. Now, it seemed that the attraction had won out—despite the fact that Mistral's behavior toward him continued to be prickly and piquing.

However, if Jordan were honest with himself, he knew that he must admit that was part of why she interested and intrigued him. He was not accustomed to being treated so by a woman. It was a refreshing change from the attitude of the glamorous, jet-setting females who regularly fawned all over him—more often than not more captivated by his money than by him.

But Mistral was ignorant of his true identity, and she didn't seem to be overly impressed by his good looks, either. It dawned on Jordan that maybe women in general wouldn't find him so desirable without Westcott International behind him. That was a thought designed to cut his ego down to size, he realized wryly.

He was actually sorry when each slice of apple pie boasted a scoop of ice cream and he had no further reason to remain wrapped around Mistral. Reluctantly Jordan released her and, carrying two of the plates, rejoined Nicabar at the table.

Beset by tumultuous emotions, Mistral pressed the lid back onto the ice-cream container, then shoved it into the freezer of her small refrigerator. She poured hot coffee for the two men, then took her own cup and plate over to the table and sat down, not daring to glance at Khalif, for fear that he would see how confused and conflicted she was. She wished that he had never come to the Big Top, that he would just go away and leave her and Nicabar alone.

But that was not going to happen—not even tonight. For, after consuming their pie, the two men settled back to linger over their coffee, Nicabar lighting his pipe and Khalif a slender cigar, while Mistral rose to finish washing the dishes, stacking them in the drainer rack on the counter to dry. The two men talked easily as they smoked contentedly together, exactly like the old friends that Nicabar had claimed that they were, their conversation covering a wide range of topics. Mistral was surprised to find that the lion tamer was extremely intelligent, well-read and informed.

It would have been so much easier for her to stifle her attraction to him, to learn what his plans for the Big Top were, if he had turned out to be nothing more than a big, dumb cluck, she thought. Because the smarter and shrewder he was, the more difficult her task of exposing him for a fraud was going to be—

especially since her grandfather was clearly so fond of him.

Long after the two men had finally bid her goodnight, Mistral lay awake in her narrow bed, mulling over the day's events and feeling as though, somehow, her entire world had been abruptly turned upside down and was now rushing headlong toward some violent cosmic collision.

Five

It's Showtime, Folks

The following afternoon was the matinee performance, and as Mistral peeked out from behind the long, heavy draperies that shielded the underground portion of the stadium from the seating, she had the invariable butterflies in her stomach. It didn't matter that she had been a circus performer for as long as she could remember or that the crowds that flocked to the Big Top were seldom large. She still got anxious before every single show. Her grandfather called it an edge that kept her on her toes. But she called it a curse. It made her worry about falling off one of the horse's bare backs or from the trapeze.

"Good," Nicabar had declared stoutly once when she had voiced her fear to him. "For it is when you get complacent that you get careless and make mistakes."

Mistral didn't know whether she agreed with that philosophy or not. It seemed to her that you were more likely to screw up if you were already a nervous wreck. But maybe her grandfather was right, after all. She hardly ever slipped up during her routines.

As usual, much to her disappointment and despair, the matinee was not a sell-out performance. At least half the seats were empty, if not more. There hadn't been time before the show to advertise the fact that the Big Top had acquired a lion tamer, and since they had played this particular arena before, it was likely that people remembered that they hadn't seen much of a circus the last go-around.

Mistral sighed heavily. It was just so hard to entertain the public these days. There was simply so much to choose from—music, sports, dance, theater, movies, books, computer and Nintendo games, the Internet—that it was almost overwhelming. And the more sophisticated the entertainment got, the more jaded and fickle it seemed that the public grew, demanding ever bigger and more elaborate thrills.

In her heart, she knew that the Big Top just wasn't exciting enough to compete. They needed more dangerous stunts—or at least showier ones—feats that would set the public to talking. Word-of-mouth advertising was always the best kind.

"Not much of a crowd, is it?" Jordan asked as he

came up behind Mistral to take a look at the stadium. "Sorry, I didn't mean to startle you," he continued when she jumped a mile at the sound of his voice.

"I didn't hear you. Do you always move so quietly, Khalif, sneak up on people like that?"

"I was hardly sneaking, Mistral. But I will admit that the combination of rubber-soled shoes and the noise in the arena aren't conducive to anybody hearing much down here. Would you say that that's a typical house out there?" He nodded toward the stadium's seating.

"Yes, it is. But then, I warned you that the Big Top was small and struggling, that we don't usually sell a whole slew of tickets to our performances. The public's just used to bigger and better things."

"Not necessarily in the smaller cities that make up the Big Top's circuit. They're usually bypassed by the big shows."

"For the most part, yes," Mistral agreed slowly. "But still, you can only play the same show on the same circuit so many years in a row before even the smaller cities get tired of you, decide that you've got nothing new to offer."

"Well, this one's in for an unexpected surprise, then, aren't they?"

"You're referring to your lion-taming act?"

"What else?"

"I—I don't know," she stammered, realizing that she had almost given away the fact that she suspected him of being full of all sorts of unpleasant surprises. "Of course you meant your lion-taming act. I suppose that I was just wondering if that's all you do...all you've ever done during your circus career. I mean, everybody in the Big Top does double duty in one way or another—"

"And you're thinking that it's hardly fair for me to receive a salary and a percentage of the gate if all that I do is my lion-taming act?" Jordan's mouth turned down sardonically at one corner.

"Yes, something like that, I guess," Mistral confessed, greatly relieved that Khalif had provided her with a reasonable explanation for her awkward question earlier. It would never do for him to learn that she believed him to be working, in reality, for Bruno Grivaldi, bent on doing whatever harm he could to the Big Top.

"Over the years, I've tried my hand at any number of acts and other jobs in the circus," Jordan said quite truthfully. "Everything from sweeping up to knife throwing to the trapeze. But you must realize that I'm far too big and tall for a lot of those things now. I'm afraid that these days, I wouldn't make a very good tumbler, for instance. But don't worry. I plan to do my fair share of setting up and tearing down equipment, and of mucking out the animal cages and trailers."

"Well, I'm very glad to hear that—because I wouldn't want to think that you were trying to take advantage of Grandpapa," Mistral dared to say, despite her misgivings at putting Khalif on his guard. "He's an extremely kind old man, and the Big Top has been his whole life, so I'd hate to see him hurt."

"Believe me, you have absolutely nothing whatsoever to fear from me in that regard." Jordan's voice was so sincere that Mistral was taken aback.

Despite herself, she couldn't help but wonder yet again if she had, in fact, made a terrible mistake in suspecting that Khalif was part of Mr. Grivaldi's plot to take over the Big Top. Unaware of her thoughts, Jordan went on.

"I promise you that I have only the best intentions where Nicabar...Grandpapa is concerned. He's been very good to me, taking me in when I needed someplace to go. I won't ever forget that. That's why I want to help him build the Big Top back up to its former status. It used to be something really special in the old days."

As he gazed down at her, Jordan thought that Mistral was something really special, too. She was dressed in an ice pink, sequined costume for the bareback-riding act, and besides being on the skimpy side, the spandex suit molded her body in a way that left little to the imagination. She had high, full breasts and a slender waist that flared into slim, curved hips and long, beautifully shaped legs that, without warning, he envisioned wrapped around him while the two of them made love. Every ounce of her was taut with graceful suppleness and muscle borne of her years in the circus.

She had her face made up, too, with theatrical cosmetics—makeup that was a good deal heavier than what Jordan was accustomed to seeing on a woman, but that, strangely, didn't appear overdone on her.

Rather, it accented her slanted cat's eyes with their
thick, sooty lashes, and her full, generous mouth in a
fashion that kept his gaze riveted on her countenance,
imagining those lips parted and gasping for breath,
kissing him, blowing in his ear, nibbling on his lobe,
moaning with pleasure as he thrust into her.

"You...you must have known Grandpapa a very
long time to be familiar with how the Big Top used
to be." Silently Mistral cursed the low, smoky breath-
iness of her voice. She didn't know what was the
matter with her.

Ever since Khalif had appeared on the scene, she
seemed to have lost control of herself and her emotions. Right now, her heart was hammering so loudly
in her breast that she thought he must surely be able
to hear it, and her body felt so weak and boneless that
she was slightly surprised to find herself still standing,
to realize that she hadn't melted into a pool of quick-
silver at his feet. She wished that he would stop staring at her as though he were a lion on the prowl and
she were a tasty, meaty morsel that he intended to
gobble up in one bite. It was doing crazy things to
her insides.

"I've known Grandpapa since I was a child," Jordan reported truthfully. "It was only later in life that
I...went overseas." Which was not exactly a lie, he
told himself, since he had, in fact, been to Europe
several times. And he intended, in his role as Khalif
Khan, to blend truth and fiction as much as possible,
since he knew from experience that falsehoods were

much more likely to be believed when intermixed with accurate information.

Circus workers carrying equipment through the passage to the floor of the stadium beyond forced him to move nearer to Mistral, so that he was almost pressed up against her, so close, in fact, that she could feel the heat that emanated from his body, smell the faint, masculine scents of the thin cigars that he smoked and the light sweat that sheened his body. Despite that the huge doors leading outside from the underground area were standing wide-open, it was nevertheless hot and humid in the arena, and Mistral felt as though the temperature had just risen a couple more degrees with the lion tamer's proximity.

"Well, I'd...I'd better go finish getting ready for the show," she said.

For one wild, frightening but equally exhilarating instant, she thought that Khalif wasn't going to step aside for her, that he actually intended to mash her up against the wall and rain hot, passionate kisses all over her, such was the glitter of his jet-black eyes as they raked her assessingly. But the moment vanished as quickly as it had come, so that in the end, as he at last moved away to allow her to pass, Mistral had to wonder whether or not she had imagined the whole thing.

It was all that she could do to compel herself not to run back to her trailer.

"Missy...what's wrong? You look like you're about to faint! Missy...?"

Realizing suddenly that she was being spoken to,

Mistral started from her daze to see her best friend, Deirdre O'Halloran, staring at her with concern.

"Oh, DeeDee, I'm…sorry. I was…lost in thought, and I didn't hear you."

"Are you all right?"

"What? Oh, yes…yes, I'm fine, really, just a little warm from the summer heat, that's all. I was on my way back to my trailer, to check my makeup before my act comes up. Do you want to go with me?"

"Sure." Blowing a bubble with her gum, Deirdre fell into step with Mistral as they crossed the parking lot to the latter's trailer. It was only marginally cooler inside, despite that Mistral had a fan running. "So, I saw you talking to the new lion tamer," Deirdre announced as she plopped down on one of the benches at the table. "Quite the handsome one, isn't he?"

"I suppose so," Mistral agreed reluctantly, taking a seat before her vanity and beginning unnecessarily to touch up her hair and makeup.

"He certainly seemed quite smitten with you, Missy."

"Oh, go on, DeeDee." Mistral grimaced wryly. "Why would he be interested in me?"

"Well, if you'd really take a look at yourself in that mirror once in a while, you might know the answer to that." Deirdre shook her head, half exasperated by her friend. "You're gorgeous, Missy."

"Oh, DeeDee, it's so sweet of you to say so. But you don't have to spare my feelings. Really. I know that I don't fit the fashion magazines' idea of beauty these days. I mean, I'm not drop-dead glamorous or a stunning knockout or anything like that. I don't look like Rachel Hunter or Elle MacPherson or any of the other supermodels.''

"Maybe not. But there's something arresting about you all the same, Missy. You've got an exotic face," Deirdre insisted stoutly.

"What you really mean is that I have a face like a cat's." Mistral smiled ruefully. "I know. It's my eyes. They're green and slanted. And I've got tawny hair, too—the same color as a tabby cat. Maybe that's why I always get hit on by all the strays hanging around the circus!"

"You get hit on because men find you attractive, Missy."

"Now, I know that you're just being kind, DeeDee. Why, if you weren't married to Liam, you'd have more dates than anybody else I know." And that was the truth, Mistral thought, sighing inwardly as she glanced at her best friend.

Deirdre was pure Irish, red haired and blue eyed, with rose-tinted, porcelain skin that boasted a dewy sheen in the summer heat. Mistral knew that try as she might, she would never in a million years look as beautiful as her friend.

"Well, don't let Liam hear you say that! You know how he is. He has a fit if any other man even glances in my direction."

"I know. It's so romantic, DeeDee. It must be wonderful to have somebody love you as much as Liam does. He's one in a million. All that I ever get are the bums...men who just want to sleep with you and

move on—or else who want to drink up your paycheck and beat you up afterward, keep you barefoot
and pregnant, with no life of your own. They've got
no brains or ambition—and that, I sure don't need."

"Not all men are like that, Missy. You said yourself that Liam was different. Certainly he wants to get
ahead in life…maybe even manage a big circus someday. I know that sounds like an impossible dream, but
you never can tell. I think that he and I would make
a real good management team together, and maybe
someday, somebody will give us a chance to prove
it."

"You already have, DeeDee. Really. I don't know
how I'd get along without you and Liam helping me
with the day-to-day operation of the Big Top."

"Shoot. You'd do just fine on your own…even
better if you had a husband to take up some of the
slack. You need to start thinking about your future,
Missy. Nicabar's getting up there in years. He can't
go on forever, and even a circus this size will be hard
to run on your own. You need a husband to look out
for you. Liam says that more than once, he's had to
step in to prevent some of the male employees from
getting bold or rough with you. You know how they
are, with their Old World ideas. They don't like taking orders from a woman."

"As much as I hate to admit it, I know that you're
right about that, DeeDee," Mistral confessed glumly.
"Mostly it's Otto who's difficult for me to handle.
He doesn't really mean any harm, I don't think.
But…well, he's just so big and strong—and he has

such a terrible temper when he gets worked up. However, since he's been with the Big Top for years, and we need him, I just can't fire him. Besides which, he does almost all of the heavy lifting.''

''Well, if you ask me, that new lion tamer could replace Otto in a minute. What's his name? Khalif Khan or something like that? He looks as though he could hold his own against anybody. Why, I don't believe that there's an ounce of fat on him. I'll tell you what. If I were single like you, Missy, I'd give him the rush for sure!''

''Deirdre!''

''Well, I would—and what's more, you're a fool if you don't. If you ask me, he's the best-looking male to happen along in ages.''

''That may be,'' Mistral conceded crossly. ''But even so, we don't know anything about him—and I'm telling you, there's something not quite right about him, DeeDee…like his joining the Big Top to begin with. A man like that, he could surely have got a position with a much bigger circus. And to tell you the truth, I'm afraid that maybe he isn't really a circus performer at all, that he works, in reality, for Bruno Grivaldi and has hired on with the Big Top in order to sabotage Grandpapa's circus!''

''Mistral, that doesn't even make any sense,'' Deirdre stated calmly. ''For one thing, Nicabar's known Khalif for years, so the man must have been a circus performer at some point in time, even if he worked other jobs during the off seasons. And for another, why would Mr. Grivaldi go to so much trouble and expense to provide the Big Top with a lion-taming act? Especially since that would only wind up hurting him in the long run, providing the Big Top with a popular, crowd-pleasing act virtually guaranteed to boost ticket sales and thereby putting the Big Top on a more solid financial footing? That would only make it even more unlikely that Nicabar would sell Mr. Grivaldi the Big Top. It wouldn't help Mr. Grivaldi at all. No, depend upon it. If that unscrupulous rogue intends some mischief to the Big Top, it will come in the form of a torch tossed into the hay in the animal trailers or else a sledgehammer taken to crucial equipment."

"Perhaps you're right, DeeDee," Mistral agreed slowly at last, seeing the logic of her friend's line of reasoning. "In fact, I'd already thought of much of this myself. But still, no matter what, there *is* some mystery surrounding Khalif. He…he just doesn't have a circus performer's hands." She was reluctant to admit that she had studied the lion tamer's hands closely, given her friend's obvious desire to play matchmaker.

"What do you mean?"

"His hands…they're smooth and well kept. DeeDee, when was the last time that you saw a circus performer who didn't have rough, callused hands? Look at your own. Look at mine. Oh, yes, I'll grant you that we try to grow decent nails and keep them nicely polished. But does that last? How long before you've got a new blister from the trapeze bar, or else you've broken a nail while dealing with some piece of equipment? Even Tanisha has fake nails."

Tanisha Ladi was the Big Top's contortionist, who performed her act with her pet boa constrictor. Her only other prop was the platform that she appeared on, fashioned to look like a huge African drum and which the male employees of the circus wheeled out on stage for her. So, of everybody who worked for the circus, Tanisha did the least amount of manual labor, although, just like everyone else, she was always ready and able to lend a helping hand whenever and wherever the need arose.

"Missy, did it ever occur to you that maybe Khalif's just vain about his hands?" Deirdre inquired. "He probably wears work gloves or something when he has to take care of his animals and equipment— and wielding a whip and a starter pistol in the center ring isn't hardly designed to exact a heavy toll on your hands, besides. You know, I think that maybe this trouble with Mr. Grivaldi has got you so worked up that you're imagining bogeymen in every corner."

"Oh, DeeDee, you've got such a reasonable explanation for everything that I just can't help but think that maybe you're right. Maybe I *am* just jumpy, making mountains out of molehills. Maybe Khalif really *is* just as vain as he is arrogant. Hell, maybe he sits in his trailer at night, buffing his nails himself because he's got nothing better to do. I don't know."

"Well, I just don't think that you ought to be leaping to wild conclusions until you *do* know, Missy." Deidre's tone was firm. "You could be missing out on a real good thing because of your suspicions—besides which, I'm glad that the man's joined the Big Top, and so is most everybody else. This circus has been without a lion-taming act for far too long. Maybe now, we'll start getting a little of the recognition and revenues that we deserve—and maybe even other, equally exciting acts will want to hire on with us, too. If you ask me, you ought to be grateful that Khalif wanted to be a part of the Big Top. After all, just as you pointed out earlier, he probably could have taken his lions anywhere. In my opinion, we're very fortunate to have got him.''

Mistral hadn't really looked at the situation that way before. Now, she realized that of course, all of the Big Top's other employees must be ecstatic at having a lion tamer on board. A circus just wasn't actually much of a show without a lion tamer, but, rather, on a par with carnivals and their barkers, sideshows and freaks—most of the latter of which, Mistral knew, were, in reality, fakes.

She didn't want the Big Top to garner a reputation of being little more than a hurdy-gurdy production, and deep down inside, she was forced to admit to herself that more than one person had viewed the circus as such, which was why it had been increasingly playing second- and even third-rate circuits.

"You make me feel ashamed of myself, DeeDee," Mistral stated quietly, stricken. "I hadn't until just this moment realized what Khalif's joining the Big Top must mean to everybody else. I know that Nicabar and I can't afford to pay you all very much, that you're just barely scraping by. Of course, if having a lion-taming act will bring in more money, I'll be more than happy to have him with us.'' Then, glancing at the small travel alarm clock that sat on her vanity, she abruptly cried, ''Oh, my heavens, just look at the time! We'd better get back to the stadium before the show starts without us. Grandpapa will never forgive us if we're late!''

Deirdre didn't need any reminding about that. Nicabar was a stickler for professional behavior—and that included being on time for a performance.

Exiting the trailer, the two women hurried across the parking lot to the arena, Mistral determinedly setting aside her misgivings about Khalif. Her best friend's sensibleness had made her feel more than a little bit foolish and overimaginative, as though she had been reading far too many mysteries and spy thrillers of late, causing her to suspect murder and mayhem at every turn.

Deirdre was right. She should be glad that Khalif had joined the Big Top. Still, as she remembered the way that his gleaming obsidian eyes had raked her appraisingly earlier in the underground passage leading into the arena, Mistral shuddered in the summer sun, her body suddenly feeling as though it were doing a slow burn.

Six

In the Center Ring

Mistral and Deirdre reached the underground passage just in time to get into their proper places in the line that had formed for the showy parade that traditionally opened the circus. Until today, Mistral had always deep down inside—although she would have died rather than to have admitted it to her grandfather—felt slightly ashamed of the Big Top's parade and wished on more than one occasion that Nicabar would simply dispense with it.

With the circus's performers doing double and even triple duty, she could maintain the illusion that they fooled the public into thinking that the Big Top was a much larger circus than it truly was, although she suspected that, in reality, at least half of those seated in the stadium knew differently. But the parade made it clear that the Big Top was only a small, struggling circus—a far cry from being in the same league as those like the Ringling Bros. and Barnum & Bailey and the Jungle King circuses.

However, her grandfather wouldn't hear of doing away with the opening parade. It was a time-honored circus tradition, he would have insisted stubbornly had she ever dared to broach the matter—and added that one did not get ahead in life by pretending to be something other than what one was, besides.

But now, as Mistral reached for the flamboyant, satin magenta cape that she had earlier left lying on a folding chair sitting in the underground passage and, with hands that trembled a little, fastened it securely around her neck, she realized that Deirdre had indeed been right, that Khalif Khan's presence was going to affect more than one positive change in the Big Top.

He was standing at the end of the line, dressed in an elaborately embroidered, flowing white burnoose that looked as though it had cost a fortune. An Arabian headdress and highly polished black boots completed his ensemble. In one hand, he carried a long, snakelike leather whip. Behind him, in a queue that even Mistral had to admit appeared extremely impressive, were the sixteen ornately painted cages that held his lions and lionesses.

They would take quite a while to navigate the oval circumference of the arena, giving the impression—

however erroneous—that the Big Top was at least twice the size that it actually was. At the realization, Mistral's heart swelled. For the first time in a very long while, as her sturdy gelding Golden Boy was led forward and, after grabbing a handful of his long, shaggy mane, she easily pulled herself onto his back, she felt a sense of anticipation and exhilaration as the stadium's lights abruptly dimmed and then a bright white spotlight flashed on to highlight her grandfather.

He was garbed in the traditional ringleader's black silk top hat and tails, with a black, red-satin-lined cape fastened at his throat and pristine white gloves on his hands, in one of which he bore a black, silver-knobbed cane. Was it only her imagination, or did he actually seem to stand a little taller and prouder this afternoon rather than stoop-shouldered and with an air of weary bravado.

"Ladies and gentlemen, boys and girls of all ages," Nicabar's voice rang out boldly through the arena's public-address system as he spread his arms wide, twirling both his cane and cape with a flourish. "We proudly welcome you to the Big Top!"

Sweeping off his top hat, he bowed low to the applauding crowd, then jammed the hat back onto his head and, as the taped music began to blare the opening number, started the long march around the concourse, grinning broadly, pumping his cane enthusiastically and lifting his knees high as he strutted and danced along, playing to the cheering house.

As she watched him, Mistral caught a glimpse of

what her grandfather must have been like in his youth, before age and worry about keeping the Big Top alive had taken their toll on him. Unexpectedly tears of joy stung her eyes. For at least that moment, her uneasiness about and resentment toward Khalif dissipated. Somehow, she knew that he had been responsible for this change in Nicabar, and for that alone, she would have given the lion tamer just about anything that he desired.

The line began to advance. Dashing away her tears and plastering a wide smile on her face, Mistral nudged Golden Boy forward. For an instant, as keyed up as she was, he snorted and pranced, tossing his plumed head, so that she was forced momentarily to grab hold of the strap that encircled his girth. But at a spoken command from her, he quieted, and then she lifted her hands high, waving to the throng as she passed by.

Unbeknown to her, from the rear of the queue, Jordan watched her, thinking to himself how she stood out in the deep, bright pink cape, her unbound hair flowing like silk in the slight breeze that wafted through the stadium, its tawny gold color matching the shade of the palomino that she rode. She sat tall and erect astride the broad bare back of the horse, and such was her seat and control that she and the animal moved as one.

She looked like some ancient goddess, Jordan thought—Epona, the Celtic horse goddess—or else some regal queen of old. Dressed in a fabulous designer gown and bedecked with the Westcott diamonds or emeralds, she would more than hold her own at any high-society bash, he mused. She would, in fact, turn heads, such was her strange, exotic beauty.

Her name was French, but Jordan believed that he also detected a hint of Slavic in her slanted green eyes and her high cheekbones with their delicate hollows beneath. It was hard to tell with circus performers; many were descended from generations of Europeans and Asians. The Big Top, for instance, was a motley mix. Regardless, there was something special and arresting about Mistral St. Michel, as though she were an atavism, a throwback to some earlier time, haunting, half savage, a graceful wild child more in harmony with nature than with the modern world.

She belonged on the back of that horse—a beautiful, breathtaking, barbarian princess riding over the Steppes. What a challenge it would be to tame her! Something told Jordan that she would not be easily won, but also that once conquered, she would be fiercely loyal to her husband, not the type of woman to stab him in the back during a board meeting or to spend her afternoons slipping off to some discreet hotel to lie with a lover. In some dim corner of his mind, it occurred to him that he could do a lot worse.

Across the stadium, as Golden Boy progressed, Mistral could feel a peculiar, unnerving prickling along her spine. Somehow, she knew without even turning her head to glance around that Khalif was staring at her, his black eyes smoldering like twin embers.

Damn the man!

What right did he have to look at her as though he were mentally stripping her naked, pressing her down upon a bed somewhere, his dark body sliding to cover her own pale one? It was unsettling, distressing…thrilling. Good Lord! Where had that last idea come from? The very last thing that she wanted or needed in her life was a man, especially one like the enigmatic Khalif Khan, who—no matter what Deirdre had said—had some mystery attached to him.

As excited as she had been at the beginning of the parade, Mistral was now equally glad when finally it ended and she was able to slip away from Khalif's hungry, penetrating gaze. It was not the first time a man had ever looked at her in that fashion. It was, however, the first time that her body had ever leaped and flamed in response. She didn't know what was the matter with her, why she should be so physically attracted to the insolent lion tamer.

Until his arrival, she had had no problems whatsoever in keeping her natural urges at bay. That was why, at twenty-five years of age, Mistral was still, incredibly, a virgin. She knew that many of her fellow circus performers would find that fact hard to believe, but it was true.

In earlier years, she had been so because Nicabar had been very strict, warning her of the consequences of premarital sex—of the sexually transmitted diseases rampant worldwide, of the effects that an unplanned pregnancy would have on her circus career, of the fact that not every man who would want to sleep with her would also want to marry her, to assume responsibility for her welfare and that of their children, and of the fact that even a husband could be brutal, abusive, faithless, a drunkard, a dope addict, a spendthrift.

"You're young, Mistral," her grandfather had told her once. "You have your whole life ahead of you. And sex and marriage are big steps. There's no need for you to rush into either. So take your time, learn how to stand on your own two feet first, how to take care of yourself, get yourself an education, and then when the right man for you *does* come along—as he unquestionably will—be sure in your heart that he loves you and that you love him before you commit yourself to him."

Mistral, her eyes opened early on by her vagabond life with the Big Top, had perceived the wisdom of Nicabar's advice and taken it to heart. But contrary to what he had said, the right man had never come along, and the more that she had seen of the world, the more convinced she had become that he never would, that, in fact, knights in shining armor had, sadly, gone out of fashion centuries ago, that, these days, there were only bums to be found.

Khalif, however, appeared to run disturbingly contrary to this mold. From what she had seen of him so far, Mistral judged him to be not only a vain and arrogant devil, but also, perversely, an intelligent, compassionate, responsible and hardworking man— which made her suspicions about him seem all the more irrational.

Backstage in the dressing rooms, Mistral hurriedly changed her costume, donning a sea green, sequined leotard and matching satin cape. But afterward, she was so lost in thought that she started when she heard her grandfather announcing the only minor act that she was in, a type of aerial ballet.

"And now, ladies and gentlemen, boys and girls, we present for your entertainment in the center ring the Tumbling Turi Brothers, and on the ropes, the Spinning Selinka Sisters."

Belatedly Mistral followed Deirdre and the other females in the act to the floor, abruptly drawing up short when she saw that Khalif, now in plain clothes, stood holding her rope.

"What are you doing here?" she asked anxiously, her voice almost a hiss. "Where's Paolo?"

Paolo Zambini, who was one of the clowns, almost invariably worked the rope for her during this particular act.

"I don't know," Jordan replied casually, shaking his head. "Nicabar just told me to come out here and handle your rope."

"Do you even know how?"

"Yeah, I do. So relax, Mistral. I promise that I'm not going to send you sailing out over the cheap seats."

Much to her outrage, the lion tamer actually grinned impudently as he spoke this last. Adding to her ire was the fact that unbidden into her mind came the thought that he had a disarmingly crooked smile that made her long to trace the contours of his sensual mouth, to press her own lips to his.

"Well, let us hope for my sake that you're telling the truth," she said as she unfastened her cape and slipped off her high heels, beginning to rub her hands and bare feet with the resin contained in a small box near her rope. "A bad injury is about the last thing that I need right now."

"Don't worry. Like I told you, I've done this before." And indeed Jordan had on many occasions during his youth undertaken this very same task for his mother whenever they had visited the circus and she had been unable to resist clambering up the rope for old-times' sake, as much a daredevil in her own way as his father had been.

Mistral knew that she had no other choice but to trust him. Her grandfather would be furiously upset if she left the floor in the middle of a performance when there was nothing seriously wrong with her. No matter what, the show went on, and many a circus performer had appeared onstage while under the weather or with a wrist or an ankle in a cast. A well-known trapeze artist of years gone by, who had performed with her bar dangling from a circling rocket, had for a stretch of time done her act with a broken leg, the limb encased in plaster all the way up her thigh.

Shooting Khalif a dark glance that spoke volumes, Mistral began to climb the thick rope. Regardless of her feelings, she couldn't afford to delay any longer. This was a synchronized act. She couldn't stand around on the floor, arguing with the lion tamer, while all of the other women were performing on their ropes.

Still, as she ascended higher and higher, her mouth was dry with anxiety, her palms were sweating and her heart pounded. What if she were right and Deirdre were wrong? What if Khalif really *was* working for Bruno Grivaldi? What better opportunity for him to cause trouble for the Big Top? If she were out of commission, then Nicabar, Liam and Deirdre would be forced to shoulder her responsibilities among them, and they couldn't possibly manage with everything else that they had to do.

In the end, however, all of Mistral's fears proved in vain. Khalif did, in fact, know how to work the rope. Indeed, he was as good as Paolo in that respect, never spinning her too fast or too slow, and keeping the rope steady as he turned it.

From below, Jordan watched her intently as she stretched and arched, did arabesques and turned upside down, the powerful, supple muscles in her arms and legs flexing, her toes gracefully pointed. Just as his mother always had, Mistral made the aerial ballet look easy. Still, he knew that it was anything but. It required superb strength and control and nerves of steel. One wrong move and Mistral could fall tens of feet, possibly even to her death. Two of the younger girls, just learning the act, worked with harnesses so that they wouldn't slip up and take that fatal plunge. But Mistral had no such protection.

Despite the resin that he rubbed on them earlier,

Jordan's palms sweated on the rope. But he didn't for even an instant release it or take his eyes off Mistral. Her life was literally in his hands. She had climbed the rope trusting and depending on him to work it properly. Prickly pear though she was, he wasn't about to let her down.

She was slipping a collar over her head now, which she would attach to the rope and with which she would do a very fast spin, hanging by her neck. As a child, whenever he had seen this done, Jordan had always marveled that the performers didn't break their necks. Even now, he was still astounded by the feat.

Mistral appeared to be an expert at it, never faltering as her voluptuous but compact body turned and turned, faster and faster, until Jordan felt dizzy just looking at her. Only, he wasn't sure that it was simply from all the spinning.

Then the act was over, and she slid quickly down a second rope that he pulled over to her for that purpose. Like any good assistant, he draped her cape around her as she slipped on her high heels.

Her body was warm and dewy with perspiration from her exertions, and for a moment, Jordan had a wild, almost uncontrollable urge to haul her into his arms and taste her full, rosebud mouth. The fragrance of her wafted enticingly to his nostrils...vanilla again, mingled with her own musky scent. For an instant, she trembled beneath his hands, as though she sensed his thoughts. And then she swiftly stepped away, smiling brightly as she curtsied and waved to the audience, and the spell that had engulfed him was broken.

Anger overtook him instead. Clearly Mistral St. Michel wanted nothing whatsoever to do with him. The realization stung Jordan's pride and vanity. It seemed that no matter that he had always been considered the epitome of tall, dark and handsome, he was having difficulty attracting a woman without his wealth and Westcott International behind him.

After her bows, Mistral strode rapidly backstage, not even thanking him or sparing him a second glance. Jordan didn't realize that this was because she had been so unnerved by having his arms wrapped around her that her only thought had been of escape.

It was not until she reached the women's dressing room and began to change back into her bareback-riding costume that Mistral recognized how well the lion tamer had handled the rope for her and the fact that she hadn't even bothered to thank him. Given her behavior toward him the past two days, he must believe that she was one of the most unforgivably rude females that he had ever had the misfortune to know. Undoubtedly she had imagined the desire lurking in the depths of his glittering black eyes, her mind transforming it from the dislike that it was, in reality.

Well, there was nothing that she could do about her oversight at the moment. She would simply have to seek Khalif out later and thank him. And actually, the fact that he had worked the rope for her had alleviated some of her fears about him, because he couldn't have known in advance that he would be

asked to do something like that. That he had proved
adept at the task demonstrated that despite her suspicions aroused by his elegant, well-kept hands, he
did, in fact, know his way around a circus.

Once she had finished her bareback-riding act, Mistral hung around in the underground passage, from
which she could watch the remainder of the first half
of the show. She wanted especially to see Khalif's
lion-taming act, which would close the show's first
half.

There was a great deal of excitement as the Big
Top's workers rushed to and fro in the semidarkness,
erecting the giant, circular cage in which Khalif
would perform. From experience, Mistral knew that
there would be many people in the crowd who were
afraid that the cage would prove too flimsy to contain
the lions and lionesses, since the cage walls would
tremble when the animals struck it while performing
their leaps and bounds.

But that was part of the thrill of the circus, part of
what attracted the audience to begin with and kept
them glued to their seats—the possibility that disaster
would strike, that an elephant would suddenly go berserk, rampaging madly through the arena; that one of
the lions or lionesses would attack their trainer, maul-
ing him; that a performer would slip and fall from the
high wire or the trapeze. This last was how her own
parents had died.

Everyone familiar with circuses also knew the
tragic history of one of the industry's most famous
families, the Wallendas, many of whom had plunged

to their deaths from the high wire. And it was not just performers who were injured and even killed. Mistral was aware of instances in which circus equipment, improperly erected by inexperienced workers, had given way, sending platforms and heavy poles toppling onto the audience, hospitalizing or killing many of the spectators.

Such accidents were a constant reminder that while the circus was every child's dream, it could also be a dangerous, even deadly profession. It took a certain type of personality to put one's life at risk night after night.

"And now, ladies and gentlemen, boys and girls, from out of the deepest, darkest jungles and the hottest, most desolate deserts of Africa, the Big Top is proud to present the savage, daring, incomparable Khalif Khan, lion tamer extraordinaire!" Nicabar's voice boomed through the stadium.

Mistral edged closer to the floor so that she could get a better view as Khalif strode into the enormous steel cage, the folds of his Arabian headdress and his embroidered white burnoose flowing. He was accompanied by Tanisha, who had evidently graciously consented to act as his assistant. Once inside the cage, he slipped off his headdress and burnoose to reveal that, beneath, he wore an ornately decorated black vest, skintight black pants and a pair of highly polished black jackboots.

Despite herself, along with the rest of the women in the arena, Mistral couldn't help but sigh appreciatively as she observed Khalif's magnificent physique.

He might not be accustomed to hard, manual labor, she thought, but he had definitely been strenuously working out in some fashion to have acquired those powerful biceps, that taut, corrugated stomach and those beautifully corded thighs. His bare chest was broad and muscular, covered with a sprinkling of fine black hair.

Unwittingly she thought of resting her head against that chest, listening to the steady beat of his heart after the two of them had made love together.

"Good Lord, Mistral," she muttered to herself. "What are you thinking of? You'd better get a grip, my girl."

With a flourish, Tanisha collected Khalif's discarded outer garments, then salaamed and exited the cage. At that point, a small door set low in one side of the cage was lifted, and from the smaller individual cages that imprisoned them beyond and that were now joined together in a long queue, the lions and lionesses bolted one after another into the huge, circular cage. Each knew its assigned place on the brightly painted platforms within and took up its position—all, that was, except for the last lioness in.

Her name was Huseina, and she was one of the two best-trained animals in the act. It was her job to provide the danger and excitement by misbehaving. This put the audience on the edge of their seats, thinking that the lioness was still wild and savage, capable of turning on her trainer at any moment when, in fact, she was one of the two least likely of all to do so.

In keeping with her role, however, Huseina

prowled restlessly around the big cage, low growls emanating from her throat and her long tail switching furiously. Khalif spoke to her sharply. Then, with a great deal of panache, he cracked his whip and pointed demandingly to her platform.

Huseina ignored him.

Again, Khalif spoke to her sternly, his whip snaking out and his hand indicating her platform. Once more, the lioness ignored him. This same scenario was enacted yet again before, at last, hissing and snarling, Huseina bounded up the platform to her proper place. But once there, she did not settle tamely into position. Instead, she opened her lethal mouth to let out a long roar. Khalif turned, as though really furious now at her behavior, and rebuked her.

At that, she swiped out at him with one powerful paw. With the butt end of his whip, he pushed her paw away. She roared once more, and this time, Khalif staggered back, broadly waving his hand in front of his face, as though she had bad breath that had nearly asphyxiated him. As intended, this drew peals of laughter from the crowd. Even Mistral, from her vantage point in the semidarkness of the underground passage, found herself smiling.

When he had apparently recovered, Khalif spoke authoritatively to the lioness again, only to receive yet another roar and a paw swipe for his pains. This time, however, when he poked the butt end of his whip at her, Huseina obediently sat up on her haunches, her forepaws raised high into the air. This was the cue for the rest of the animals also to sit up, which they did. When all of the big cats were poised on their haunches, the audience applauded enthusiastically.

Despite herself, Mistral had to admit that Khalif was good—far better, actually, than she ever expected. His tall, dark, handsome looks didn't hurt, either. He might indeed have stepped straight out of a Berber tent. From the very first moment that he had entered the cage, he had had the crowd eating out of his hand. There was a vibrancy and appreciation about them that Mistral hadn't felt from a crowd in quite a while.

Deirdre was right, she realized then. The lion tamer *was* going to be quite good for business—maybe enough of an addition that other important acts *would*, in fact, want to join the Big Top. For the first time since she had fully grasped the small circus's desperate financial straits, Mistral felt as though perhaps there actually *was* a light at the end of the tunnel.

Khalif continued his act, putting the lions and lionesses through their paces. His other best-trained big cat was a lion named Fadil. His job was to be the pussycat. He did a multitude of tricks, including rolling over, purring loudly and then sitting up and kissing Khalif on the nose, much to the audience's delight.

At the end, one by one, the lions and lionesses exited the giant cage the same way as they had entered it. The only one who stayed behind was Huseina, still pretending to give Khalif a hard time. Shouting and cracking his whip, he chased her all

PLAY
RUN
FOR THE
ROSES

(banner — obscured)

and get
THREE FREE GIFTS!

HOW TO PLAY:

1. With a coin, carefully scratch off the silver box at the right. Then check the claim chart to see what we have for you — **FREE BOOKS** and a **FREE GIFT**—**ALL YOURS FREE!**

2. Send back the card and you'll receive two brand-new Silhouette Desire® novels. These books have a cover price of $4.25 each, but they are yours to keep absolutely free.

3. There's no catch. You're under no obligation to buy anything. We charge nothing — ZERO — for your first shipment. And you don't have to make any minimum number of purchases — not even one!

4. The fact is, thousands of readers enjoy receiving books by mail from the Silhouette Reader Service™. They like the convenience of home delivery...they like getting the best new novels months before they're available in stores...and they love our discount prices!

5. We hope that after receiving your free books you'll want to remain a subscriber. But the choice is yours — to continue or cancel, any time at all! So why not take us up on our invitation, with no risk of any kind. You'll be glad you did!

This surprise mystery gift
Will be yours **FREE** –
When you play
RUN for the ROSES

The Silhouette Reader Service™ — Here's how it works:

Accepting free books places you under no obligation to buy anything. You may keep the books and gift and return the shipping statement marked "cancel." If you do not cancel, about a month later we'll send you 6 additional novels, and bill you just $3.49 each, plus 25¢ delivery per book and GST.* That's the complete price — and compared to cover prices of $4.25 each — quite a bargain! You may cancel at any time, but if you choose to continue, every month we'll send you 6 more books, which you may either purchase at the discount price...or return to us and cancel your subscription.

*Terms and prices subject to change without notice.
Canadian residents will be charged applicable provincial taxes and GST.

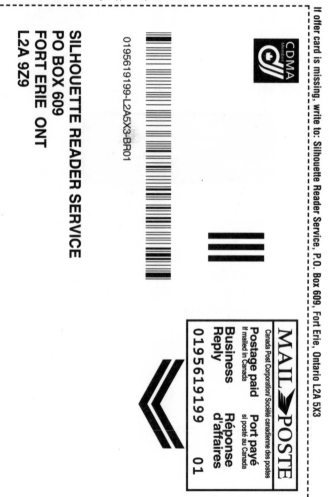

If offer card is missing, write to: Silhouette Reader Service, P.O. Box 609, Fort Erie, Ontario L2A 5X3

SILHOUETTE READER SERVICE
PO BOX 609
FORT ERIE ONT
L2A 9Z9

019561919199-L2A5X3-BR01

CDMA
Member

Canada Post Corporation/Société canadienne des postes
Postage paid   Port payé
If mailed in Canada   si posté au Canada
Business   Réponse
Reply   d'affaires

01 9561919199   01

MAIL ▶ POSTE

around the cage—to no avail. She went on refusing to leave the cage.

Finally, hissing and roaring, she suddenly pivoted and bounded straight toward him, as though she were going to attack him. It all looked so very real that even Mistral, along with the rest of the crowd, felt her breath catch in her throat, experiencing a seemingly interminable, utterly horrible moment of fear and morbid expectation at the thought that Khalif was about to be mauled to death.

But with a swiftness that was incredible, he jerked his pistol from the belt at his waist and fired at point-blank range at the charging lioness. The shot seemed to explode into the now deathly quiet of the stadium. Then, there was an audible, collective gasp as the lioness skidded to an abrupt halt, then toppled over and lay still.

The tension that filled the arena then was almost palpable. Mistral knew that although the audience was trying to reassure itself that what they had just witnessed was only an act, they nevertheless half believed that Huseina had gone berserk and turned on Khalif, and that he had killed her.

Khalif himself was a master showman. For fully a minute, he didn't move, didn't even twitch a muscle, just stood there, smoking gun in hand, staring at the lioness, heightening almost unbearably the tension that had built in the stadium. Huseina herself was superb. Not by even so much as a flick of her long tail did she reveal the fact that she was actually still alive.

At last, shoving his pistol back into his belt, Khalif

walked toward her. Bending down, he made quite a display of checking to ensure that the big cat was dead. Then, grunting, his muscles bulging and straining at the effort, he heaved her onto his shoulders—no easy feat, Mistral knew, since a fully grown lioness like Huseina could weigh almost five hundred pounds. The big cat continued to play her part like a true professional, hanging limply around his shoulders.

For a breathtaking instant, it seemed as though Khalif would stride from the enormous cage without letting the crowd know that it had all been just an act. But then, at the last minute, he reached up and scratched the lioness's ears affectionately. That was her cue, and she knew it. Raising her head then, she gave him a very long, sloppy lick across his cheek to show that it had all been just a game.

The audience went wild, cheering and applauding and stamping their feet, so that the entire arena appeared to shake as though collapse were imminent. Nodding and waving to the crowd and still carrying Huseina, who now purred and switched her tail contentedly, Khalif exited the huge cage and headed toward the underground passage.

Spying him approaching, Mistral hastily stepped back against the wall, wary of him and the lioness both. Her heart lurched uncontrollably in her breast as, seeing her standing there, Huseina hissed and spit at her.

"Don't be alarmed," Jordan said reassuringly as his gaze took in Mistral's wide eyes, the pulse fluttering wildly at the hollow of her throat. "That's what all lionesses do when they like you."

"*Like you?*" she echoed, with trepidation. "What do they do when they *don't* like you?"

"They go for your jugular without any warning. That's why I myself prefer the females who hiss and spit." *Like you,* Jordan almost added, but didn't.

Nevertheless, he felt certain somehow that Mistral had heard the unspoken words, because although there was no room left for her to step back any farther, she flattened herself against the wall, one hand flying involuntarily and protectively to her throat, as though to ward him off.

Unable to resist, he shot her an insolent, knowing grin.

Roughly, reminding him of her presence, Huseina licked his ear—and then she growled again at Mistral, just as any other jealous female would have.

Seven

Sweeping Up After the Show

It was as though the success of Khalif's lion-taming act had rejuvenated the Big Top, Mistral thought as she left the now-empty stadium, walking slowly across the parking lot to her trailer. The second half of the show had, if anything, been even better than the first, the trapeze act, which was the grand finale, actually living up to its dramatic billing as the Spectacular Solanas. Somehow, every difficult stunt that they had attempted—and that normally went poorly, sending the trapeze artists free-falling to the safety net below—had instead this afternoon been completed in championship style.

Mistral knew that, this afternoon, she and the rest of the Solanas could have held their own against any other trapeze act in the world.

When he had closed the show and thanked the audience for coming, upon Nicabar's weathered face had been such an expression of heartfelt joy that Mistral had nearly wept. She had not seen her grandfather look so happy in a very long while. His voice had quavered with emotion as he had expressed his gratitude to the crowd.

Afterward, backstage, he had hugged Mistral tightly.

"This afternoon...this afternoon was just like the old days, my dear," he had told her. "I could see...on the faces of the children, I could see that we had made the magic of the circus come alive for them. Even the adults knew that there was something special about today's show."

"Yes, Grandpapa, I believe that they did," Mistral had concurred.

Now, inside her trailer, she stripped off the dazzling, cerulean cape and sequined leotard that she had worn for the trapeze act. Then she carefully zipped all three of her costumes into a garment bag to protect them and hung them on the clothes rod in her closet. Her shoes, she tucked into plastic shoe boxes and placed on the closet shelf.

She wished that she had a bathtub, into which she could have poured a generous portion of bubblebath liquid, then lain back and soaked her aching limbs. But her trailer didn't boast anything fancier than a cramped shower. She turned on the taps and, once the water was warm, stepped beneath the weak spray. What she wouldn't give, just once, for a shower with enough water pressure to sluice through her long, thick hair like the proverbial hot knife through butter.

Someday, Mistral thought, she was going to give up this gypsy way of life, get some kind of a corporate job and move into an apartment—a proper home without wheels. She would have not only incredible water pressure, but also a hot-water tank large enough that she could stay in the shower for hours if she wanted. She was going to have a real kitchen, too, not just a narrow galley, and a real bedroom with a fine canopy bed.

The only entertaining that she was going to do then would be the kind where you had a houseful of guests for dinners and parties. She would set such gorgeous tables and cook such fabulous meals that people would compare her to Martha Stewart. Maybe she would even start up her own magazine. She had a knack, a flair, a natural instinct for interior decorating and design. Everybody said so—and Mistral knew that they weren't just being kind. She thought that she could manage one of those home-and-garden magazines, one like she was always reading.

"Get real, Mistral," she chided herself crossly as she finished rinsing off the vanilla-scented soap with which she had generously lathered her body. Grabbing a towel and wrapping it around her wet, naked body, she exited the shower. "You don't really know anything about anything except running a circus.

Who's going to hand you a job publishing a magazine, based solely on your word that you've read hundreds just like it over the years and have a good eye for style? Nobody, that's who. You're dreaming, my girl—a lovely, lovely pipe dream. You don't even have a college degree. Your computer skills are minimal. You'll be lucky to get a position as a receptionist, answering telephones all day!''

Annoyed at herself, roughly she toweled her body dry. Then she tossed the towel onto her narrow bed— only to snatch it up moments later, jerking it around herself again as there came a knock at her trailer door.

"Who—who is it?" Mistral called.

"It's Khalif."

Good grief! It was the lion tamer, and she was standing here stark naked, with only a towel to preserve her modesty.

"Could you...could you give me just a minute?" she asked. "I'm—I'm not dressed."

"That's okay. I don't mind," came the insolent reply, making Mistral long to box his ears soundly.

"Well, I do. So you can either hang around outside until I can get something on, or else you can get lost, buster!''

Much to her fury, Khalif's response was a burst of low laughter.

"What's so funny, you arrogant devil?" she huffed.

"The fact that you trusted me to handle your rope when your life was at stake, but that you *don't* trust me to come inside your trailer when only your modesty is in question.''

Mistral bit her lower lip agitatedly, torn. When he put it that way, it really *did* sound ridiculous.

"You can at least wait until I slip on my robe," she insisted finally. "I just got out of the shower, and I've only got a towel wrapped around me."

"That, I'd like to see."

"Well, you're not going to get the chance, so forget it!''

Whirling, she strode to her closet, yanking a pair of lacy panties from one of the drawers inside, stepping into them so awkwardly in her haste that she stumbled and nearly fell. Then, hauling her robe off the clothes hook on the inside of the door, she pulled it on. Her heart was racing, and her hands trembled as she drew the robe closely around her and tied its long sash as tightly as she could.

Really, it was purely stupid for her to be so unsettled and embarrassed, Mistral thought. The costumes that she performed in were far more revealing than either the towel or the short robe that she now wore. Still, her breath seemed to come far more shallowly and rapidly than it ought, as though she were hyperventilating. Trying to force herself to breathe more normally, she at last opened the trailer door.

Khalif stood on the steps just outside. He had obviously showered and changed clothes, as well, since he was now wearing a pair of blue jeans and a black T-shirt with red graphics and white lettering that read: Area 51, The Ultimate Dreamland. Once You Enter,

You Can Never Leave. His gaze swept her from head to toe.

"It was definitely worth the wait," he announced, causing her to blush furiously.

"I'm busy," she hissed. "What do you want?"

"Grandpapa has invited me to be a permanent guest at your dinner table. But when I asked him if he'd checked with you about that, he said no. He seemed to take for granted the fact that I'd be welcome. However, I don't want to impose. So I thought that I'd better find out for myself whether or not you had any objections. For whatever it's worth, however, I don't have any intentions of being a mooch." He indicated two brown paper sacks, which she had not noticed before, that sat on the steps at his feet. "I bought groceries."

For a moment, Mistral felt a rush of anger at her grandfather's presumption. Then she remembered what Khalif had done for the Big Top today, and she deliberately swallowed the hotheaded reply that she had been about to make.

"I—I don't know what to say. I'm afraid that you've taken me by surprise."

"Say that it's as easy to cook for three as for two— and that I needn't think that I'm going to get by with only bringing two bags of groceries."

"I—I suppose that depends on what's in them. Won't you...won't you come in, Khalif?"

"Now, that's the best offer that I've had all day."

Hefting the two sacks, he followed her inside. Setting the bags down on the kitchen counter, he began to take out their contents. Mistral could hardly believe her eyes. She was accustomed to savory and filling but inexpensive fare...stews, soups, spaghetti, goulash, macaroni and cheese, ham and beans, salads and breads. Khalif, however, clearly possessed a much more sophisticated palate.

Her mouth fairly watered as her startled gaze took in his purchases—a pot roast, a Virginia ham, T-bone steaks an inch thick, Cornish hens and beef kabobs. And that was just the meat. He also produced fresh vegetables—asparagus, new potatoes, broccoli, carrots, tomatoes, mushrooms and spinach. There were different kinds of lettuce, as well—romaine, butter and endive—and two specialty breads.

"I didn't know what you liked, so I just chose a variety," Jordan told her. "I went for a short walk after the show, and I discovered quite a nice little grocery store only a few blocks from here. I hope that everything's okay."

"Okay? It's wonderful. It's...it's far too much, in fact," Mistral admitted reluctantly. "Look, Khalif, I don't want to pry, but, well...how can you possibly afford all this?"

"I...ah...thought that Grandpapa had explained all that to you. Over the years, whenever there was an off day for the circuses that I performed with, I scrounged around town for any extra, temporary employment that I could find...running errands, yard work, you name it. If it was honest labor and meant a few additional dollars in my pocket, I took it. I saved all that I could and started to invest it—first in a friend's small business, and then later, as I got older and more knowledgeable, in things like stocks, bonds and mutual funds. I'm not a rich man, by any means," Jordan lied. "But between my investments and the circus, I have a comfortable enough living that I can afford to splurge now and then."

"I see." The wheels in Mistral's brain churned furiously. Here, perhaps, was a way for her and Nicabar to save the Big Top! "Khalif, I've got a little money set by—for emergencies. It's not much, but, well...do you think that you could help me, teach me about the financial market? I'm not stupid, and I've got a fairly decent education from all the books that I've read over the years. But despite that I've tried on my own to figure it out, I'm afraid that high finance merely confuses me. If I could learn, however, I could help Grandpapa with the circus. It's...well, you must know that it's on pretty shaky ground financially right now. One unexpected major expense could wipe us out."

"I...guess that I didn't realize that things were *that* bad," Jordan answered slowly, disturbed. "I mean, Grandpapa said that he had some problems, and I knew that they were worse than he ever let on. But I thought that the main threat to the Big Top was external...Bruno Grivaldi and the Jungle King Circus."

"Mr. Grivaldi is nothing more than a shark who sees us as easy prey—which we are at the moment." Mistral's face was grave, and her mouth trembled vulnerably as she spoke. "But if we had a better income, we could attract bigger acts and crowds, and then Mr. Grivaldi wouldn't find us so defenseless. I just

couldn't bear to see Grandpapa lose the Big Top. It's
been his dream, his whole life. Oh, I don't even know
why I'm telling you all this! It isn't your problem. I
watched you this afternoon. Your act's good.
No…it's fabulous. If the Big Top folds, you won't
have any trouble at all getting employment with some
other circus. In fact, I imagine that you could just
about take your pick. I don't know what ever made
you choose the Big Top to begin with!''

"I told you. I owe Grandpapa, and I want to help
him out.''

Jordan had realized as she had talked that Mistral
wasn't really nearly as feisty and hard-edged as he
had originally supposed. Her attitude was only a shell
that she had built around herself to protect herself
from the cruelties of the world. He should have recognized that fact sooner, he chided himself, annoyed.
Circus life wasn't easy. As a result, its people were
a closed lot to outsiders, naturally suspicious of
strangers. He knew that.

"I'm more than willing to teach you about the
stock market, Mistral,'' he continued. "But even so,
I'm afraid that you won't find it the quick fix that
you're hoping for. Financial investments can be extremely risky, and starting small, you won't make a
whole lot of money in the beginning. It might take
years for you to build up a viable portfolio.''

Jordan felt bad for putting a damper on her dreams,
especially when her arresting face, which had just moments before been bright with hope and expectation,

now fell, the light in her green eyes dying and her mouth acquiring a wry, bitter twist.

"Yes, of course you're right. I—I should have realized...." Her voice slowly trailed away. Mistral felt like a fool. Doubtless, Khalif would now not only think her ill-mannered, but also a complete ignoramus. "Look, I'm sorry. I really didn't mean to burden you with all of the Big Top's problems. They're not your concern. I...ah...appreciate your offer to help me, and I don't mind starting small. In the meantime, I guess that I'll just continue to try to stave off our creditors as best as I can." She paused, then abruptly changed the subject. "I want to thank you, as well, for the groceries—and for working my rope this afternoon."

"Don't mention either. They were both my pleasure. So...what time's dinner?"

"I'm going to start it right now. We've got another matinee tomorrow—in another small city," Mistral explained. "So we'll have to drive all night to make it there with plenty of time to spare in order to set up before the show."

"Right. Why don't I just give you a hand in the kitchen, then?" Jordan suggested casually.

"That—" *That won't be necessary,* Mistral had started to say. But to her surprise, what came out instead was, "That would be real nice, Khalif. I'd appreciate that."

Her heart beat fast at the gorgeous, crooked grin that she received in response. She didn't know why she should suddenly feel so lighthearted, as though things were not so very bad, after all. But she did. It was irrational and inexplicable. But there it was all the same.

Eight

On the Road

Much to her surprise, in the days that passed as the Big Top continued its summer tour, Mistral found herself spending more and more time with Khalif. At first, it was only supper in her trailer almost every evening, and since Nicabar was present then, too, she could assure herself that she was doing nothing more than humoring her grandfather by being cordial to someone whom he obviously looked on as a surrogate grandson.

There was nothing wrong with that, Mistral told herself. She had been foolish to think that just because Nicabar apparently doted on Khalif, he would stop caring about her, that Khalif would take her place in her grandfather's heart. Helping a great deal, too, to alleviate her fears in this regard was the fact that one night after dinner, when Khalif had left the two of them alone together, Nicabar, puffing contentedly on his pipe, had begun to talk to her fondly about the old days, when the Big Top had been a circus of some note.

Then, after a while, he had sighed and said quietly, "Mistral, you know that ever since your parents died when you were just a child and I took you in, you have been as a true granddaughter to me. I want you to know that nothing in the world could ever change that. So you don't have to worry that Khalif would ever supplant you in my affections. That's the nice thing about hearts, you see. They have a boundless capacity for love of all kinds."

"I know that, Grandpapa. I learned that at your knee, watching how you cared for all the Big Top's employees as though they were your own family," she had replied, feeling her heart lift nevertheless at his reassurance—and ashamed that she had ever doubted his love for her.

Taking her mind off that wholly unwarranted but still nagging worry, too, was the fact that the Big Top had begun to suffer a series of small but disturbing mishaps—flat tires and overheated engines on various of the vehicles; missing sacks of feed for the animals, among other lost supplies; damaged costumes and equipment.

At first, the incidents were such that despite all of

her suspicions, Mistral knew that they could have been nothing more than accidents. Most of the Big Top's vehicles were old, prone to the problems of age. It was also easy enough to misplace supplies, what with the constant loading and unloading that was an everyday part of circus life. Costumes and equipment, too, had been refurbished many times over the years, so that it was not unreasonable to expect that sooner or later, they would wear out.

Still, Mistral was upset, certain that, somehow, Bruno Grivaldi was at the root of all the Big Top's troubles. She could not help but think that it was strange that all of the mishaps had begun occurring after Khalif had joined the circus. But even she couldn't reconcile the great popularity of the lion tamer's act with Mr. Grivaldi's possible sabotage.

Word-of-mouth advertising about Khalif had successively increased the Big Top's audiences at each new city so much that it was hard to see how he could possibly be aiding Mr. Grivaldi's cause. While the accidents were a drain on the circus's financial resources, they were being more than offset by the rise in ticket sales. Logically, then, that pointed either to the lion tamer's innocence and the fact that the problems were the result of sheer bad luck, or else to the idea that the culprit responsible for the mishaps was someone other than Khalif.

This last notion dismayed Mistral no end, because except for the lion tamer, the Big Top didn't have anybody new working for it. Yet it was difficult to see how the mischief—if that was indeed what it

was—could have been carried out by an outsider.
That meant that someone that she and Nicabar had
known and trusted for years was betraying them. This
was an utterly horrible thought, one that, to her deep
shame, made Mistral even suspect her best friends,
Deirdre and Liam O'Halloran, because Deirdre had
mentioned that her and Liam's dream was to manage
a circus. Had Mr. Grivaldi promised Deirdre and
Liam management of the Big Top in exchange for
their assistance in forcing Nicabar out?

"No, I just can't believe that," Mistral muttered
angrily to herself as, with a pitchfork and shovel, she
continued the job of mucking out the horse trailers,
which she had undertaken earlier that morning. "I
won't believe it!"

"You won't believe what?" Jordan asked, curious,
as he came up behind her, causing her nearly to start
out of her skin. "Sorry," he apologized. "I didn't
mean to scare you. I know that it must seem like it
since I frequently appear to catch you unawares, but
I really wasn't trying to sneak. You must spend quite
a bit of time so lost in thought that you're oblivious
of your surroundings, Mistral. Worrying about the circus again—or should I say still?"

"Yes." She bit her lower lip as she dug her shovel
into a pile of horse manure and then emptied it into
a nearby plastic bag. Many circuses made extra
money by sacking and selling their animal manure to
avid gardeners on their circuits, and the Big Top was
no exception. It was a little known aspect of the industry, but one that served the circuses well. "It just

seems as though too many things have gone wrong lately for it to be mere chance.''

"You might be right about that, actually. Here, you hold that bag open for me.'' Reaching out, Jordan pried the shovel from her grasp and began to employ it himself industriously. "Do you have any ideas as to the identity of the culprit—or am I the only person on your short list of suspects?''

"*Should* I suspect you?'' Mistral inquired, only half-jokingly.

Jordan shrugged. "It would be natural enough under the circumstances. I mean, I *am* the new kid on the block, and it's difficult to see how if there *is* a saboteur at work, he—or she—could be an outsider, not since Nicabar warned the entire troupe to be on the watch, anyway.''

"Yes, I know. I've thought about all of that. But it...doesn't really make sense for you to be harming the Big Top in some way. You'd be doing us a lot more damage simply by quitting and taking your lion taming off to some other circus.''

"Well, I'm glad to know that even if you *did* suspect me, you decided that I really didn't fit the bill. So who else did you consider?''

"No one, really.'' Mistral blushed furiously as she saw one corner of Khalif's sensual mouth turn down sardonically.

"Of course you realize that you're one of those people who gives herself away whenever she tells a lie, don't you?'' he prodded mercilessly.

"Yes. However, it's very ungentlemanly of you to

point that out. If you'd been decent, you would have accepted my statement at face value and left it alone.''

"But, then, I never claimed to be decent, did I?" Jordan grinned at her insolently, his black eyes sweeping her body from head to toe, in a way that caused the crimson that stained her cheeks to spread and deepen.

She wore a pale green T-shirt whose hem, because of the summer heat, she had gathered up and tied in a knot just beneath her breasts, baring her flat, taut midriff. A pair of tight blue jeans encased her long, graceful legs, and sturdy boots were upon her feet. She had her long tawny hair swept up and secured with a banana clip. Because of her strenuous exertions, she was sweating profusely. Strands of her hair had come loose to hang in damp, sexy tendrils around her heart-shaped face. Perspiration trickled from her temples and beaded her pouty upper lip, giving her porcelain skin a dewy glow. Her T-shirt was soaked through, the thin cotton fabric molded to her breasts in a fashion that revealed her bra beneath, leaving little to the imagination.

Even as Jordan stared at her, he saw that Mistral had grown painfully aware of his gaze and of its provocative, predatory nature. Of their own volition, her nipples had tightened, straining against her bra and T-shirt, so that he could discern the twin peaks clearly.

She was so fair skinned that they would be as rosy as her blush, he thought. He imagined them naked, taut, upthrusting, swelling against his palms, as firm as ripe cherries in his greedily imprisoning mouth, his tongue taunting them, licking them, tasting and savoring their sweetness. The erotic pictures in his mind caused his sex to grow achingly hard—a fact plainly exposed by his own tight blue jeans, and of which Mistral was not unaware, he realized.

"I've—I've got some—some other work to—to do," she stammered in a rush, beginning to move toward the open doors of the horse trailer.

Of its own accord, Jordan's left arm shot out, slamming against the wall of the trailer, blocking her escape.

"What's your hurry?" he drawled softly. "We're not even half finished here yet."

Mistral didn't know what to say or do. Her heart was hammering so hard that she was terrified that it was going to burst from her breast. She felt as though she were on fire inside, molten, melting, all her bones dissolving within her. Her breath came in short, shallow gasps that sounded overly loud to her in the tension-filled trailer, as though they roared in her ears. Her head reeled as though she suffered from heatstroke, and she was about to pass out. Worst of all, a strange, burning ache had seized her between the thighs, and she felt a sudden rush of warm moisture there.

Panic caught her in its grip. It seemed to her that the trailer, which could carry up to four horses, had shrunk horribly in size, that Khalif loomed over her like some barbarian desert warrior, bent on taking by force whatever he desired. She imagined him tossing her down upon the straw that carpeted the trailer floor, stripping off her clothes and spreading her thighs wide to push his way inside her.

To her utter astonishment and mortification, some treacherous part of her was not wholly appalled by this scenario, but, rather, thrilled and tempted by it, knowing that it would fill and ease the scalding, hollow sensation that had taken possession of her. Swiftly she lowered her gaze, not wanting Khalif to see the confusion and possible consent there. But it seemed that he must have seen, anyway, because before she realized what he intended, he had captured her jaw in his strong, slender hand, tilting her face up to his, his mouth swooping to claim her own.

Although Mistral had been kissed before in the past, those kisses had been nothing compared to this. This kiss was unbelievably expert, with a wealth of experience behind it. Somehow, she knew that instinctively even as it overpowered her senses like some narcotic, shattering her and leaving her dazed, unable to think, only to feel.

Khalif's lips were hard, hungry and demanding. They seemed to devour her, to swallow her breath, to drain the very life and soul from her body and then to pour it back in. She felt so weak in her knees that she knew that she would have fallen had he not held her so tightly, his powerful arms crushing her against him so that she could feel the heat that emanated from his whipcord body, the sweat that sheened his dark flesh.

He smelled of masculine scents, tasted of masculine tastes that intoxicated her with their very maleness and unfamiliarity. His long, elegant hands had slid up her back to her nape, and then to the clip in her hair, pulling it free and tossing it aside. Now, his fingers snarled roughly in the tawny, silken mass, holding her still for his invading tongue that plunged deeply into her mouth, probing every moist, dark crevice, tangling with her own tongue.

In some dim corner of her mind, Mistral knew that she ought to resist, to push him away instead of drawing him even nearer, her hands creeping up of their own volition to wind convulsively around his neck, her fingers burrowing through his long, glossy black hair that was like waves of silk when she caressed it. She hadn't known that it would be so thick, so soft.

She wanted to feel his head pressed to her breasts, his hair brushing across their twin peaks. She longed to feel his lips there, too, teasing and tasting her nipples. As though cognizant of her thoughts, her breasts swelled against him, their tips rigid and straining, begging, aching to be fondled.

The feel of them pressed against his chest almost drove Jordan crazy. Some part of him recognized that he was moving far too fast, too soon. But he couldn't seem to stop himself. One hand swept down to cup her right breast, kneading and squeezing, so that the thin cotton of her T-shirt and bra rubbed across her nipple, stimulating it unbearably, dragging a low moan from her throat.

The sound inflamed Jordan. Jerking his mouth from

hers, he tugged her head back and pressed his lips to the slender column of her throat, searing the length of it. His tongue darted forth again to stab the tiny pulse fluttering wildly at its hollow.

Mistral felt as though a powerful electric shock had just jolted through her. Instinctively she hungered for more. She had never felt like this before. She seemed to have lost her ability to speak, even to reason, was instead being carried along helplessly in the wake of Khalif's onslaught upon her body and senses.

A little voice in the back of her head whispered that this was all wrong, that she would regret it later. But she paid it no mind, feeling that she couldn't have heeded it even if she had tried. The emotions and sensations that had her fast in their grip were too strong, too overwhelming for her to combat. Even her fear of where this might be leading was not enough for her to put a halt to Khalif's encroachment upon her.

It was as though something inside her had been sleeping, waiting all her life for this moment, and now that it had been wakened by his kisses and caresses, it refused to return to its previous state of dormancy. Instead it pulsated through her body, rousing, stirring. Vaguely Mistral understood that no man had ever really kissed her, touched her, broken through her reserve until now.

Somehow, Khalif had managed to do that. She didn't know how or why he should have been the one to accomplish that. She hadn't even known him all that long or well. But from the first moment that she had ever seen him—climbing down from the cab of his sixteen-wheeler—she had felt some magnetic attraction to him. Still, she had attempted to fight against it. But now, it was irresistibly pulling her in.

She just couldn't let that happen, she realized as, suddenly, all of Nicabar's warnings returned to haunt her. She didn't know in her heart that Khalif was the one and only man for her. Certainly, despite that they had been spending more and more time in each other's company, he had never spoken of a relationship between them—much less of loving her. And she herself was still conflicted in her emotions toward him, uncertain of her feelings.

Other than her own line of reasoning, she actually had no basis for not believing him to be the person sabotaging the Big Top. Even Khalif himself had admitted that, being the newest addition to the circus, he was the likeliest suspect.

"No...don't," Mistral murmured as, his mouth still scorching her with each kiss, he lowered his head to her breast. Abruptly regaining her senses, she began to struggle against him, attempting to push him away. "You—you mustn't. I'm so sorry. I—I don't know what got into me. I wasn't expecting anything like this. You—you took me by surprise. I'm so sorry," she repeated lamely, gasping a little for breath, feeling as though she had just run a very long way and could not now get enough air into her lungs. "I—I just can't do this."

Jordan's breath, too, came in harsh rasps as he stared at her, momentarily uncomprehending. Then, slowly, it dawned on him that Mistral was rejecting his overtures. It had been a very long time since something like that had happened to Jordan Anthony Westcott. At first, as worked up as a lathered horse and desperately wanting an outlet for his passion, he was stung by her refusal to accommodate him. Then, after a minute, the irony of the situation struck him and he threw back his head and began to laugh.

Of all the reactions that she had thought he might have, that Khalif would actually laugh at her had not even occurred to Mistral. She was shocked, dismayed, angered by his reaction. The kisses that had seemed to have caused the earth to move beneath her feet appeared not to have affected him at all. He was just like every other man whom she had ever known— using her, toying with her affections, the kind who, once he had got what he'd wanted, would have left her high and dry and probably pregnant on top of it all!

Thank God she had told him to stop when she had! Otherwise, he would undoubtedly have her down upon the hay-strewn floor even at this very moment, taking her virginity. Perhaps he would even have boasted about it to the other male performers in the circus! Everyone knew how prickly and particular she was when it came to men. She would have been a complete laughingstock, sniggered at behind her back, her very authority over the Big Top brought into question at every single turn!

Mistral's blood boiled. Without her even being aware of it, she lifted one hand to smack Khalif straight across his all-too-handsome, laughing face, intent on teaching him a lesson that he would not soon forget! How dare he think that she was some cheap, easy tramp to be trifled with and then dumped without a second thought?

Even worse, maybe there had been something wrong with the way in which she had kissed him, responded to him—something that had revealed to him her lack of experience, the fact that she was still a virgin. If that were indeed the case, no wonder he was laughing at her!

Her palm, however, never connected with Khalif's dark visage. More rapidly than Mistral would ever have believed possible, his own hand shot up, grabbing her wrist in midair and effectively halting her attack upon him. He didn't hurt her, but neither did he release her. And when she tried to hit him with her other hand, he caught that one, too, inexorably forcing her up against the trailer's wall and pinning her wrists on either side of her thrashing head, despite how she struggled against him.

"Stop fighting me, Mistral," Jordan muttered huskily as his gaze took in the expression on her face, a combination of fright and fury. Her eyes flashed emerald sparks at him, but in their depths, shadows lurked, and her mouth—bruised and swollen from his kisses—was tremulous. Her body shook with the force of her emotions. "As much as I'd like to do otherwise, I promise that I'm not going to do anything that you don't want me to do. And I'm very sorry that I laughed, since you obviously misunderstood. I wasn't laughing at you—but, rather, at my own damned arrogance.'' He smiled ruefully. "It's...well, it's been a long time since a woman told me no. That's all. It was...something of a novel experience, I'm afraid.''

"Well, in that case, I can't imagine what kind of women you've been hanging around with,'' Mistral snapped indignantly.

"You know something? I've been wondering that very same thing for quite a while now. I guess that's why I've been so attracted to you, why I couldn't stop myself from kissing you and...and... I knew that it was too much, too soon. But...the truth is that you're like nobody that I've ever known before, Mistral. In a lot of ways, you remind me of my mother.''

"Your mother?''

"Yeah. You'd like her, I think. And she'd like you.''

"Where is she?''

"She...she lives in Chicago, actually. She used to be a circus performer, too, until she retired to marry my father.'' Jordan saw no reason not to reveal this information. After all, he was supposed to have been connected with circuses since childhood.

"And what does your father do?''

"Nothing now. He died five years ago.''

"Oh, I'm—I'm sorry. I didn't mean to pry.''

"No, it's okay. He...ah...performed a lot of daredevil stunts, like Evel Knievel, and he was accidentally killed during one of them.''

"That's kind of how I lost my own parents,'' Mistral explained, her agitation slowly beginning to dissipate. "Something went wrong with the trapeze one night, and they fell to their deaths. That's why Nicabar has a strict rule about us always working with a safety net, and why he took me in. He's not truly my grandfather, you see—at least, not by blood. But I— I didn't have any other family, and nowhere else to go. So I don't know what I'd have done without him. I couldn't love him more if he *were* my biological grandfather. That's why I've just *got* to help him save the Big Top. So...if you don't mind, I really need to get back to work here."

"Yeah, I *do* mind, actually," Jordan confessed reluctantly. "But I would never do anything to hurt you, Mistral. I hope that you know that."

"I...don't know what to believe anymore—except that I feel certain in my heart that all the mishaps that we've been having lately are the work of someone who wishes to cause the Big Top so much trouble that Grandpapa will be forced to close down and sell out to Bruno Grivaldi."

"Then we'll just have to find out who the culprit is, won't we?" Jordan asked, releasing her at last, stepping back and retrieving the shovel that he had dropped when he had taken her into his arms.

Strangely enough, instead of feeling relieved by his action, Mistral was oddly disappointed. Deep down inside, she knew that if she were honest with herself, she must admit that it had been exciting, being kissed by him.

"I don't see how it's going to be possible to uncover the identity of the person responsible for all of our difficulties,'' she responded to Khalif's declaration. ''Grandpapa has already warned the entire troupe to be on the lookout, and no one seems to have noticed anything unusual.''

''Nevertheless, there will be something out of the ordinary somewhere,'' Jordan insisted, knowing from past experience that this was invariably the case. ''However, it probably won't be anything to attract attention, obviously. It might even be something as small as a change in somebody's routine or attitude. Who's hard up for money right now, so that they would be vulnerable to temptation if a man like Bruno Grivaldi offered them a tidy sum to sabotage the Big Top?''

''Everybody in the circus is low on funds. They always are. In case you hadn't noticed, we weren't exactly attracting major crowds until you came along, and although you've certainly helped the Big Top to draw a lot bigger audiences, it takes time for word-of-mouth advertising to spread. So, while our revenues are up since your joining the circus, almost all of the extra money's had to go to pay overdue bills and the repairs caused by all of the mishaps. And in the end, those may be due to nothing more than the fact that much of what the Big Top owns is old and simply succumbing to everyday wear and tear. I may just be seeing shadows that don't really even exist.'' Mistral sighed heavily.

''I doubt that.'' Jordan shook his head. ''You've managed the day-to-day operation of the Big Top for quite a while now, and you're not stupid. Over time, if they're any good at their jobs at all, people develop an instinct for them, a sixth sense about what's normal and what isn't. Clearly you don't believe that what's happening is usual—and your gut is telling you that it isn't due solely to a dreadful run of bad luck, either. Is that right?''

''Yes. But I really hate what's occurring—not only because it might force Grandpapa to shut down the circus, but also because it's making me suspect terrible things about people whom I've known for years, people who have been not just my friends, but also the only real family that I've ever had. And I—I just can't believe that one of them has turned on us, has sold out to Bruno Grivaldi!''

''That's because you're caring, conscientious and loyal, Mistral—and while those are excellent qualities, much to be admired, they're not shared by everybody else in the world. Unfortunately, when it comes to money, there are a lot more people out there who would be willing to sell even their own mothers downriver for a buck.''

''That's...that's terrible—and an extremely cynical view of the world.''

''Maybe so, but it's still a pretty damned realistic one, as you'd know if you'd been around more.''

''What do you mean? I've traveled with the Big Top since I was a child. I've been all over the place.''

''Yeah.'' Jordan nodded his agreement. ''But that doesn't mean you're a worldly sophisticate. You're not. In many respects, Grandpapa's sheltered you a great deal, so that's why you've got what I call a black-and-white mind.''

"And just what, pray tell, is that supposed to mean?'' Mistral inquired huffily.

"What it means, my girl, is that to you, people are either good or bad. You don't see any shades of gray. That's why it's so hard for you to accept the fact that somebody employed by the Big Top may have betrayed you and Grandpapa, sold out to Bruno Grivaldi. To you, they're all like family. You don't want to think of any of them as being bad people.''

"And just what's wrong with that?''

"Nothing—except that it isn't exactly an attitude designed to help you catch whoever is behind all of these seeming accidents,'' Jordan said pointedly. "But don't worry. Unlike you, I *have* been around, and I've seen what the world is like, how people behave when there're power and money at stake— which is why I've become so very jaded and cynical, as you called it. I assure you that I have no trouble whatsoever thinking ill of everyone.'' He grinned to take the sarcastic sting from his words, to show that he was at least half joking. "Besides which, I haven't known the Big Top's employees all my life. As you are aware, circus careers aren't big on longevity, and the performers who were with the Big Top when I was a kid have long since retired. So I don't have any sentimental notions clouding my judgment about the Big Top's employees, and I'm not an easy man to fool, in any event. That's why I promise you, Mistral, that we *will* learn who is behind all of this.''

Although she knew that she had absolutely no good reasons whatsoever to trust him and perhaps every basis for suspecting him as being the culprit himself, Mistral couldn't help but have faith in Khalif's words. Something deep down inside of her wanted to trust him—and not just because he was tall, dark and handsome, and had kissed her with a passion that had overwhelmed her, either.

The lion tamer was much bigger and stronger than she was. He could easily have flung her down upon the hay-layered floor of the trailer and forced himself upon her, clapping his hand over her mouth to stifle her screams. Realistically speaking, in such an event, there would have been little that she could have done to save herself. But instead, when she had asked him to stop, to let her go, he had. No matter what, she knew that on some level, then, he was a gentleman.

Besides, what other choice did she have, really, but to trust him? Mistral asked herself slowly. She couldn't watch everybody in the circus twenty-four hours a day, and she already knew that Nicabar wasn't going to be of any assistance to her. If anything, he would be hurt and upset if he ever learned that she even suspected any of the Big Top's employees of being in league with Bruno Grivaldi. Nor, despite their long friendship, could she afford to confide in Deirdre and Liam O'Halloran after Deirdre's comments about the couple's dream of someday managing a circus.

"Thank you, Khalif, for your help," Mistral said— even as she wondered if she weren't making the biggest mistake of her life by trusting him, depending on him, if she would turn out to be the simple shepherd who had opened the gate to let the big, bad wolf into the sheepfold.

Nine

Sparks and Spangles

Despite all her misgivings about trusting Khalif, Mistral discovered to her dismay that she could not help but be drawn to him more and more as the Big Top progressed along its summer circuit. For one thing, she had no one else to confide in about the ongoing mishaps that she increasingly suspected were the work of a saboteur. Although she would have liked to believe that the so-called accidents were the result of nothing more than the circus's dilapidated condition, her gut instinct kept insisting that not even the Big Top could have fallen prey to such a run of bad luck. She hated herself for even considering that one of the circus's employees was responsible, but there did not seem to be anyone else to blame.

Nor, however, did it appear possible to catch the culprit in an act of sabotage. Despite how she and Khalif both tried to keep a wary eye on things, it was impossible for them to watch every single aspect of the Big Top for twenty-four hours a day. And whoever was causing the damage was careful, seemingly taking no chances on being discovered. They would never find out who it was, Mistral thought dismally. Nor did she stand a chance in hell of earning enough money to haul the circus out of its deep financial hole.

It was all hopeless, she told herself, at her wit's end as she tossed her pencil down on top of the notebook in which she had been entering stock information from the newspaper. Khalif, who had begun teaching her about the stock market, had said that she was learning its ins and outs relatively quickly. She secretly feared that he was just being nice to her, despite the fact that she *was* showing a profit on paper, though she didn't have any actual funds invested. In her small emergency cache, she really hadn't had enough money for that, Khalif had explained to her.

So what was she doing sitting here at her table, wasting her time with all these imaginary financial maneuvers, anyway? Mistral asked herself tiredly. She ought to be outside, prowling around the trailers and hunting down the culprit who was harming the Big Top! But she made no move to leave the table. Instead, she gazed out the open window, grateful for the slight breeze that wafted indoors. It was hot outside, and even hotter inside her trailer, her one small fan doing little to cool the air.

She could feel the perspiration beading her forehead and upper lip, trickling down the hollow between her full breasts. Her red cotton T-shirt stuck to her skin, its front damp with her sweat. Her bra chafed her from the heat. At last, she stood and went into her cramped bathroom, where she stripped off her shirt and the offending bra. Bending over the sink, she wet a washcloth and sponged herself off, letting the tepid water stream haphazardly over her bare breasts, not caring that it ran down to soak the waistband of her cutoffs.

As she studied her reflection in the mirror, Mistral thought about Khalif kissing her. He had done that quite a lot since that afternoon in the horse trailer, catching her when she least expected it and claiming her mouth hungrily with his. Whenever he did so, he stroked and teased her body, too, so that despite herself, she was feverishly aroused, clinging to him and making low whimpering sounds in her throat. Now, at the memory, she felt her nipples tighten almost painfully, and a slow, melting warmth seeped between her thighs, causing her to ache there.

She didn't know what was the matter with her. Her emotions were so confused and conflicted that she hardly even knew what to think these days; she had been under such a strain. She ought not be carrying on with Khalif this way, she chided herself sternly, letting him worm his way into her confidence and press his increasingly urgent advances on her. After all, no matter that logic dictated that he was worthy of her trust, he might, in reality, be working for Bruno Grivaldi and trying to shut down the Big Top. But somehow, where Khalif was concerned, Mistral could no longer seem to exercise any kind of caution or control. He was so handsome and attractive, so experienced in ways that she wasn't, that she was finding it increasingly difficult to resist him.

Still, she tried—and Khalif knew that. He even teased her about it, making her feel uncomfortable, as though she were behaving like a child instead of a grown woman with desires and needs—both of which appeared to have burgeoned lately beyond her control. Even now, at the thought of Khalif, her nipples pebbled even harder, as though cold water trickled over them. Flushing, Mistral abruptly turned off the taps. Then, after briskly toweling herself off, she pulled her T-shirt back on, sans bra.

The brief sponge bath and stripping off of her bra helped some in the summer heat, but not much. As she sat back down at the table, she still sweltered in her trailer. She didn't want to acknowledge the fact that, in reality, the late-afternoon sun beating down on her roof had relatively little to do with how hot she was, how her attention kept straying from the stock information in the newspaper. Deep down inside, Mistral knew that if she was to be honest with herself, she had to admit that she couldn't concentrate because she was listening for Khalif.

He usually came around about this time every day, to go over the stock market with her, after which he invariably assisted her with preparing supper. During all this, he would talk to her, tease her, snatch kisses from her whenever he could, leaving her breathless, her pulse racing, no matter how hard she tried to fight against her emotions. Even now, as she heard Khalif's boots hit the steps of her trailer, Mistral could feel her heart beat with excitement and anticipation. He rapped on the door. Then, without waiting for a response, he opened it and stepped inside.

Swiftly, so that he wouldn't see how she had been listening intently for his arrival, Mistral bent her head over the newspaper and her notepad, fidgeting with her pencil.

"Well, you appear to be quite hard at work," Jordan observed by way of greeting when she failed to glance up at him. "How's it going?"

"Okay, I guess," Mistral replied, glad that her long mane of tawny hair concealed her face from him so that he wouldn't suspect that she had actually been sitting at the table, daydreaming about him. "It's— it's so hot this afternoon that I'm—I'm having a little trouble concentrating," she confessed reluctantly, aware of how little she actually had to show for all her supposed efforts.

"Yeah, the temperature's got me all hot and bothered, too," Jordan declared, fully cognizant of the fact that his words held an intentional double meaning. Rather than taking a seat opposite Mistral, he slid in next to her on the built-in banquette, deliberately laying one strongly muscled arm along the back of the bench so that it rested casually against her shoulders, and pressing his thigh up against hers. "I've hardly been able to concentrate all day."

This last was, in fact, no lie. Jordan felt as though he was going crazy, thinking about her and how she kept putting him off, letting him kiss her, then pulling away. Under different circumstances, he would have labeled her the worst sort of tease. But as he got to know and care about Mistral over the passing weeks, he was instead all too aware of how conflicted her emotions were toward him. Despite everything, she *was* attracted to him. But she still wasn't sure that she could wholly trust him; and on top of that, she had been alone for so long that she was having a difficult time convincing herself that she had a place for any man—particularly him—in her life.

Still, Jordan felt confident that he would eventually overcome all these obstacles to their relationship, that his determination and persistence would win out over Mistral's insecurities.

"So...theoretically...did you make a profit today?" He nodded toward her newspaper and notepad.

"Yes."

"Show me."

Mistral was painfully conscious of Khalif's proximity as she explained her imaginary investments, what had led her to choose the various companies that she had "bought" stock in, and the "earnings" that she had achieved. His long, lean, hard body reminded her of one of his big male cats—powerful, supple and incredibly sexy. His thigh, pressed against hers, was making her skin tingle all over. She was acutely cognizant of the fact that, earlier, she had discarded her bra. The cotton fabric of her T-shirt seemed to rub enticingly against her bare breasts, causing her nipples to peak.

As Khalif gazed down at her, she saw his eyes smolder and darken as he became aware of the fact that she wasn't wearing any bra, that her nipples were straining against the thin material. He was going to kiss her. Mistral knew that. Her heart began to hammer even more alarmingly in her breast than it had before. Involuntarily, she wet her lips with her tongue. At the unconsciously erotic gesture, Khalif inhaled sharply. Then, abruptly, his mouth swooped to capture hers, his own tongue plunging deep.

At first, Mistral tried to resist the kiss. But as usual, she was helpless against it, her mind and will seeming to melt away as his lips moved insistently on hers. His tongue traced the outline of her mouth, then insinuated itself inside again, searching out her most secret, sensitive places, tasting and teasing. Of their own volition, her arms wound around his neck, drawing him even nearer. Her fingers burrowed through his sleek, shaggy mane of black hair, tightening convulsively as he deepened the kiss, his lips growing harder, more urgent.

Groaning, Jordan clasped her trembling body to him possessively. His hands roamed over her sensuously, taunting and caressing her in the ways that he knew aroused her, gliding slowly over her breasts, rubbing the cotton of her T-shirt against them, knowing how the fabric would stimulate her nipples, sending waves of pleasure through her. Her low moan of delight in response to his tantalizing touch inflamed him. Easing her T-shirt upward, he exposed her naked breasts to his avid gaze, then lowered his head to catch one rigid nipple lightly between his teeth.

Mistral whimpered again as his tongue stabbed her with its heat. But when Khalif's hand began to slide down her belly, beneath the waistband of her cutoffs, she was abruptly jolted from her daze of delight. "No," she breathed, grabbing hold of his hand. "No, Khalif, we—we can't. It's—it's almost time for supper, and Grandpapa will be here any minute."

Jordan sighed heavily at her words, then managed a rueful grin. "I'm sorry, Mistral. You're right, of course." Once more bending his head, he brushed her lips with his, then tugged her T-shirt carefully back into place. "I wouldn't want Grandpapa to walk in on us and think I was trifling with you. Because I'm not. I want you to know that, Mistral. I'm serious about you. In fact, I've never felt this way about a woman before."

Mistral flushed, half with pleasure, half with anxiety. "I—I wish I could believe you, Khalif. But the truth is that I know you're—you're much more experienced than I am, and that men often say things to women that they don't really mean. Grandpapa's warned me about that more than once."

"Yes, and it's true," Jordan agreed, stroking her hair gently. "But whether you believe me or not, Mistral, I have no reason to lie where you're concerned. You're beautiful, and I really *have* come to care for you. So I'm willing to wait for you to be certain about that in your own mind. It's just…hard…touching you, tasting you and wanting you so badly. However, I'll deal with it. I realize you're relatively inexperienced—and that you've got a lot of other things on your plate at the moment, too. Still, you can't blame me for longing to hold you, to have you and to take care of you, Mistral.''

He kissed her tenderly again, and Mistral wanted so badly to trust and believe him that she ached inside. Logically, she recognized that it didn't make sense that Khalif was working for Bruno Grivaldi. So in her heart of hearts, she knew that the only thing holding her back now was her own fear. She didn't want to wind up being made a fool of, and no matter what else he might be, Khalif was a man who had doubtless had more than his fair share of women. Perhaps, in his own fashion, he really *did* care for her. Still, he hadn't mentioned either love or marriage, not even a committed relationship—and how could she settle for anything less?

Ten

Flying High

Despite that, like Mistral, Jordan felt certain that someone was, in fact, sabotaging the Big Top, he was nevertheless having the time of his life. He couldn't remember the last time that he had felt so happy and carefree. Although, when running Westcott International, he worked out regularly at the tony sports club to which he belonged, he very seldom had any call whatsoever to perform any kind of manual labor. Instead all of his challenges were mental, which in many ways, he had always thought, were far more stressful and cause for burnout than physical endeavors.

Thus, although not to his surprise, but much to his amusement, he was finding it a sheer delight to drive his sixteen-wheeler, to perform in his giant lion cage during each of the Big Top's shows, to muck out the smaller, individual cages of his lions and lionesses and to lend a hand whenever needed at loading and unloading equipment, helping to set it up, to tear it down and even to repair it, when necessary.

Other than the occasional telephone call to either his private secretary or his uncle Chas to find out how Westcott International was coping during his absence, he hadn't given the global enterprise a second thought—much more absorbed in the microcosm of events that was unfolding before him. He had, until now, forgotten what it was like to have few or no worries beyond when you were going to receive your next paycheck.

The trailer in which he currently lived was smaller than the walk-in closet of the master bedroom in his penthouse apartment in Chicago. And there was nobody but himself to take care of it, to keep it clean and tidy, either—although Jordan had never been prone to slovenliness. In fact, he rather enjoyed washing the few dishes that he used when he didn't dine with his grandfather and Mistral.

But most of all, those shared suppers were the highlights of his day. He had never dreamed that he could be so powerfully attracted to any woman as he was to Mistral St. Michel. Perhaps precisely because she had made no attempt whatsoever to win his favor, he had bestowed it upon her. However, he had to move carefully, Jordan knew.

Seemingly casual questioning of his grandfather—although he suspected that Nicabar had not been in the least fooled by his feigned nonchalance—had elicited the fact that Mistral had never been given much to dating, much less had a serious boyfriend.

"Her life has hardly been ideal," his grandfather had explained, "losing her parents when she was just a child and having no one but me to take her in. I tried to teach her what I could, to give her a good set of moral values, to protect her from those who might have abused her. You know the kind of men who are often to be found lurking around a circus, Jordan...lowlifes, losers, hangers-on...men who lack money and an education, who know little more than getting drunk on Saturday night and settling their arguments with their fists. Over the years, Mistral has grown into a fine young woman, with a good heart. She deserves better than that, something more than just a man who will take what he wants from her and move on."

"Yeah, I agree," Jordan had said slowly—because the truth was that he really hadn't until that moment given much thought to the fact that being a part of the Big Top was, for him, merely an interlude out of time, that at the end of the summer, he would go back to his old life, to being the president of Westcott International and all that entailed.

Much to his surprise, instead of looking forward to that prospect, he had found himself suddenly gripped by a deep sense of dismay and emptiness. He had grown accustomed to working side by side with Mistral, to hearing her thoughts, to seeing how her bright, quick mind grasped each new idea that he presented to her, how she mulled it over, wrestled with it and came to her own conclusions—even if they were contrary to his own.

He had been amazed by how rapidly under his guidance that she had come to understand the basic concepts of the stock market, about which he had begun to teach her, and how she laughed like a child with delight when they checked the newspaper and discovered that the stocks that she had invested in on paper, purely as a training exercise, had increased in value.

She was so fiercely determined, so certain that if only she worked hard enough, she could turn what little extra cash that she could somehow manage to scrounge together into a sum large enough to save the Big Top for their grandfather. She thought nothing of herself, of the fact that she didn't even own a decent dress, or that she worked long, hard hours, with little time off for herself. She didn't want to accept the fact that Nicabar might lose the Big Top, despite how she would fight tooth and nail against that.

But Jordan knew—and he had already used his vast knowledge of global enterprise to take a number of legal steps to ensure that Bruno Grivaldi was put out of business for good. Jordan had the best private detectives money could hire working around the clock to dig up whatever dirt there was to be found on Mr.

Grivaldi—besides which, he had learned that Mr. Grivaldi was not only extremely greedy, but also badly overextended financially as a result of his attempts to drive his competitors out of business one way or another.

Jordan had seen Mr. Grivaldi's type before, in many a corporate boardroom. Mr. Grivaldi was a shark interested only in making a fast buck. His business practices were shady at best, illegal at worst.

A call here and a call there, and Mr. Grivaldi was soon finding out that the banks with which he had done business in the past were now adamant about not only *not* providing him with any more credit, but also about the fact that they would no longer carry him financially by extending his outstanding loans, which would henceforth be called when due.

Jordan felt quite sure that Bruno Grivaldi had by now begun to feel the same sense of nagging worry, even panic, that had gripped Mistral and Nicabar when they had realized that their unscrupulous competitor was after the Big Top. But unlike Mistral and Nicabar, Mr. Grivaldi didn't have a Jordan Anthony Westcott to fall back on, didn't have in his bag of tricks the riches and resources of Westcott International and the fact that no bank wanted to hack off the president of that global enterprise—who might be so enraged as a result that he would withdraw his millions from the bank.

No, Mr. Grivaldi and his Jungle King Circus were currently in an even more precarious position than Mistral, Nicabar and the Big Top!

Jordan nearly laughed aloud at the thought. Rarely had he felt so much satisfaction as he did now at the idea that if everything went as he planned, he would presently be the new owner of the Jungle King Circus.

But of course, like any shark that had had the great misfortune to be harpooned, Bruno Grivaldi wouldn't go down without a vicious struggle. He would guess that somebody extremely powerful was after him— the banks would hardly have been influenced otherwise—and he would be desperate to find out the identity of his nemesis.

No doubt toward that end, he was even at this very moment calling in every marker and favor owed to him. It would be only a matter of time until he discovered that his enemy was none other than Jordan Westcott, and then only days, perhaps even hours until he learned the connection between Jordan Westcott and Nicabar Danior, since Sophia had never made a secret of her circus background.

Once Mr. Grivaldi uncovered all of that, he would attempt to see Jordan, only to be informed that Mr. Westcott was out of the office on an extended vacation. Eventually it would occur to Mr. Grivaldi that there must be some reason why Jordan had suddenly become so interested in the circus business, and he would figure out Jordan's whereabouts. Jordan had no doubt that at that point, Mr. Grivaldi would alert the media, in the hope of making Jordan appear to have lost his senses, and the media would descend in full force on the Big Top.

But before that happened, Jordan fully intended to

have found a way to win Mistral's heart, since he had become quite certain over the passing weeks that he couldn't live without her, and he very much feared that she would have nothing whatsoever to do with him if, before then, she learned that he was, in reality, not a mere lion tamer at all, but the president of West-cott International.

Now, he grinned ruefully to himself at the thought of how his uncle Chas would tease him upon finding out that he had proved no more immune than any other male in his family to the infamous Westcott "romantic streak." But Jordan's secret delight didn't last long when, rounding the corner of one of the trailers parked in the lot of the stadium at which the Big Top was currently playing, he spied Mistral standing toe-to-toe with the strong man, Otto Wetzler.

Otto's pugnacious face was as dark as a thunder-cloud, and he loomed over Mistral threateningly, one fist upraised and shaking as though he actually meant to strike her as he stood there, shouting at her.

In that moment, Jordan absolutely saw red.

Rage and fear both boiled up so furiously in Jordan that he was practically steaming as he strode deter-minedly toward the two.

"What in the hell do you think you're doing, Otto?" he asked in a deceptively soft, icy tone that would have warned anybody at Westcott International that there was about to be hell to pay. "Step back! Step back immediately, or suffer the consequences!"

"Butt out, Khalif!" Otto snarled. "This ain't none of your affair! I don't got to take no orders from no damned woman—nor stand here and be insulted, neither. I done worked for the Big Top for pert near twenty-five years, and Missy ain't got no call to stand there and accuse me of sabotaging our equipment—especially when all that I was doing was trying to fix the blasted winch!'' Otto glared at Mistral savagely, his breath coming in labored rasps. But at least he was no longer shaking his fist at her and acting as though he intended to punch her—or Khalif—in the nose.

Unfortunately Mistral couldn't say the same for Khalif. She had never before seen him angry, and she was even more frightened by the sight than she had been by Otto towering over her, bellowing like a bull at her. Khalif's eyes were as hard and cold as the obsidian that they resembled, narrowed and glinting like shards as he stared challengingly at Otto, clearly unintimidated by the strong man.

This was an entirely new experience for Otto, who, because of his size and strength, was unused to anyone standing up to him. Much to Mistral's surprise, Otto didn't behave as though he wanted to take the lion tamer on, either.

"I didn't damage the winch," Otto instead insisted mulishly. "I found it here, broken, and I was only trying to repair it when Missy happened along to say that I had betrayed her and Nicabar, that I was working for Bruno Grivaldi. I don't got to suffer such insults, I tell you. What she said ain't true. I might not like taking orders from her or any other a woman, but my loyalty is with the Big Top."

"All right, then. Let's say that you're telling the truth," Jordan stated coolly. "When you found the broken winch, was there anybody else around?"

"No." Otto shook his head. "At least, I didn't see anyone, just the winch lying here on the ground, like it had accidentally fallen out of the back of the truck. I know that it's an important piece of equipment, that we need it for putting up some of the things like the high wire. So I didn't know how anybody could have been so careless as to have let it drop out of the truck to smash upon the ground. I figured that whoever had done it got scared when they saw that it was broken, and that they had run away, not wanting to be blamed, to perhaps have the cost of the repairs taken out of their wages."

"I wouldn't have done that," Mistral protested, mortified. "I know that accidents happen."

"Yeah," Otto agreed. "But lately, we have had more than our share, it seems, and we all know that the Big Top has money troubles. You are made of sterner stuff than Nicabar, Missy, and you don't want him to lose the circus, besides. So…maybe you start cracking down on us, no?" The strong man shrugged. "It is what many of us have been expecting, anyway."

Mistral was stung and hurt that the people whom she thought of as her friends, her family, should have believed her capable of putting herself and Nicabar first, of squeezing the Big Top's employees to save the circus. Why, the performers and all the rest *were* the circus! Without them, there wouldn't be any circus worth saving!

"I wouldn't do that," she reiterated firmly. "I...apologize, Otto, if I falsely accused you of breaking the winch. It's just that...well, you're right. There *have* been a lot of mishaps lately, enough to make me think that someone at the Big Top doesn't have the circus's best interests at heart. So when I saw you standing over the winch—"

"You just naturally assumed that I had deliberately damaged it." Otto's voice held a trace of bitterness. "I am sorry, too, Missy—sorry for thinking that all of my years with the Big Top counted for something, when, obviously, they don't!"

"Oh, Otto, that's not true, and you know it. You're a valuable part of the circus. I'm...well, I'm just on edge, that's all, and you're always challenging my authority, complaining about having to take orders from a woman, when you know that the instructions that I give you are no different from what Nicabar himself would tell you to do. It's annoying and humiliating, Otto. I'm not a child anymore."

"Well, perhaps you are right," the strong man conceded with ill grace. "Now, unless you plan on siccing your boyfriend there on me, leave me be so that I can get on with fixing this busted winch!"

"B-b-boyfriend...?" Mistral echoed, startled and flushing with embarrassment as she glanced at Khalif and saw the desire and amusement that glittered in his black eyes. "You—you have...quite mistaken the matter, Otto."

"Have I, indeed?" He snorted with disbelief.

She didn't know what to say to that, and so in the end, she said nothing, merely turned on her heel and walked away, heading toward her trailer, dismayed. Was that what the entire circus thought—that Khalif was her boyfriend? Was that the impression that all of their suppers together, the time that he had spent with her, teaching her about the stock market, had given to everyone else? Didn't they know how hard she was working, trying to save the Big Top?

She didn't have time for a romantic relationship, even if she had wanted one—which she most assuredly did not! Mistral insisted stoutly to herself. The pleasure that she took in Khalif's company, the way that her heart had come to leap with joy whenever she spied him, how her skin tingled whenever he touched her, how her mouth burned whenever she remembered how he had kissed her that time in the horse trailer—those were nothing more than emotions borne of the gratitude that she felt toward him for helping her, Nicabar and the Big Top.

Although deep down inside, Mistral knew that she was lying to herself, she stubbornly refused to admit that fact. She didn't want to have fallen in love with Khalif. However handsome and magnetic, he was still only a lion tamer in a small, struggling circus, despite all of his years in the business, when, with all of his talents, he could have accomplished much more than that. So, surely, no matter what, then, he lacked ambition. Perhaps, if he were to marry her, he would turn into a man who expected to live off of her paycheck.

That this conclusion that she had drawn was extremely erroneous and did not fit her perception of his character at all, Mistral also refused to acknowledge. And when thoughts of the two of them managing the Big Top together after their grandfather's retirement occurred to her, she determinedly shoved them from her mind.

Khalif had said nothing to her to indicate that he wished them to be anything other than just friends. That he was attracted to her, that desire for her shone in his black eyes whenever he looked at her was nothing more than wishful thinking on her part, a complete figment of her imagination!

"Mistral." Jordan grabbed her by the wrist, bringing her to a halt. "We need to talk."

"About what?"

"About what just happened back there, for one thing. What made you suspect that Otto had broken the winch?"

"I told you. He was standing over it, and there wasn't anybody else in sight. What else was I supposed to think?"

"It didn't occur to you to ask for an explanation first before accusing him of sabotage?"

"Are you telling me that I was wrong?"

"Yeah—because you were."

"Well, when I want your opinion, I'll ask for it," Mistral snapped, flushing with guilt, knowing that Khalif was right, that she had jumped to conclusions.

"You just did. Now, what's all this about? I don't believe that you'd truly judge a man guilty without any proof that he had committed a misdeed."

For a moment, Mistral did not reply, biting her lower lip and feeling deeply ashamed of herself—because from the start, had she not judged Khalif and found him guilty until he had seemed to prove his innocence to her? She had, in fact, suspected everyone, seen shadows in every corner.

"It just...it just seems like everything has gone wrong lately," she confessed at last, tears suddenly stinging her eyes. "Bruno Grivaldi is like some hell-hound nipping at our heels. All of these accidents keep on occurring. You were right. I don't have enough money to invest in the stock market to have even a prayer of earning enough to save the Big Top. I never...I never even know who is going to handle my rope for me during the aerial ballet, whether it will be you, Paolo, or somebody else. Paolo always seems to be busy somewhere else—and that never used to happen. Everybody in the Big Top used to know his or her assigned place during showtime and to be there. I just...I just feel as though everything is coming apart at the seams...."

Much to her dismay, unable to hold back her tumultuous emotions any longer, Mistral abruptly burst into tears, sobbing as though her heart would break. Such was her upset that she was hardly aware of Khalif cursing softly under his breath, then drawing her into his arms and leading her to her trailer so that she would not be seen crying by the other circus performers.

Once Jordan got her inside, he sat her down on the bed.

"Mistral, you're not perfect. You're not Superwoman," he said gently. "You can't save the circus, manage it, perform in it, fix all of its equipment and make the right judgment one hundred percent of the time. Nobody could. You've driven yourself way too hard these past several weeks, and I blame myself for letting you do so, for not seeing how mentally and physically worn down you were getting."

"It wasn't your problem," she sniffled woefully against his shoulder. "So why should you care?"

"Well, you see, that's the trouble," Jordan told her, stroking her hair soothingly. "I *do* care. I care very much, in fact. And somehow, I think that you care, too. Do you, Mistral?" His voice was low, husky with emotion.

Initially, he wasn't sure that she had answered him, whether she was merely weeping so hard that it only seemed as though she had nodded her head. But then he heard her voice, very soft, choke out, "Yes, I care. I shouldn't, but I do."

"And why shouldn't you?"

"Because."

"Because why, sweetheart?"

"Because I want to make something out of myself in life. A career as a circus performer won't last forever, you know, and so I've got to plan ahead for my

future. I don't need any entanglements, hindering me
from reaching my goals.''

"You don't think that maybe I could be of help to
you?" Jordan suggested, biting his tongue to keep
from blurting out the fact that he was a multimillionaire, the president of Westcott International, that he
could assist her in becoming anything that she wanted
to be.

"I don't see how—except, of course, teaching me
about the stock market. I've really appreciated that,
and maybe someday, I'll have some money to invest
in it for real—not just on paper. But the rest I've got
to do on my own. You've got your own life to lead
and your own career to think about. Why, you might
even wind up in Las Vegas—like Siegfried and
Roy.''

"Somehow, I doubt that." Jordan smiled with
amusement at the thought. "But if I did, wouldn't you
like to come along with me? We could work together.
After all, we've made quite a team this summer,
haven't we? And you've spent so many years taking
care of other people. Don't you think that it's about
time that somebody took care of you for a change,
Mistral?''

"I can take care of myself," she insisted stubbornly.

"I know that you can, honey. But I wouldn't be
much a husband to you if I didn't take care of you
myself, now, would I?''

At first, Mistral wasn't sure that she had heard him
right.

"D-d-did you say...*husband?*" she asked, startled and dashing her tears away.

"Well, believe it or not, I'm kind of an old-fashioned guy. I think that when two people love each other, they should get married. Don't you?"

"D-d-did you say...*love...married?*"

"Mistral, one of us has suddenly acquired a stutter—and I don't believe that it's me. Am I moving too fast for you, sweetheart? I was that day in the horse trailer, I know. That's why I've tried to take things more slowly since, not to rush them. But the truth is that I'm going crazy thinking about you, Mistral, dreaming about you, being with you day in and day out, and not touching you. I *want* to touch you, to kiss you, to make love to you. And I want the right to do all of that whenever I wish. I want you for my wife...."

Unwittingly Mistral's lips parted with surprise and expectation, her breath catching on a ragged little gasp, as she saw Khalif's eyes darken abruptly with passion. It was the only warning that she received before his mouth closed over hers possessively. He kissed her slowly, deeply, his lips moving sensuously on hers, teasing, tasting. When she did not demur, he traced the contours of her mouth with his tongue, then insinuated it into the warm, moist cavern, searching, savoring, exploring every secret crevice within.

Mistral moaned low in her throat, inflaming him, and the pressure of his lips increased, grew more demanding, until she was clinging to him and kissing him back, unable to quite believe what was happening to her, the words that Khalif had spoken to her, the way that he was kissing her, as though he would never get enough of her. She was half-afraid that she was only dreaming, that she would awaken at any moment to discover that none of this was real, but was only a product of her vivid imagination.

She trembled with swiftly spiraling passion and need in his strong embrace, feeling as though she were losing control of herself, that her capacity for reason was being thoroughly routed, until she could no longer think at all, only feel. Her body had become a quivering mass of exquisite sensation, pulsing and leaping in response to his hands that roamed over her, deftly divesting her of her T-shirt, her bra.

Her pale, full, ripe breasts sprang free, burgeoning with desire, their crests already taut and rosy, begging and aching to be touched.

"You're so beautiful, Mistral," Jordan muttered hoarsely against her throat as he pressed her down upon the narrow bed in her trailer. "I think that I've wanted you from the very first moment that I ever saw you standing there in the parking lot that day I joined the Big Top. The sunlight was spilling over your hair, making it look like spun gold, and your eyes flashed so like emeralds that all I could think about was stripping you naked and draping your body with jewels before making love to you."

His hands swept down, brushing across her nipples, causing waves of electric pleasure to radiate through her entire body and wringing more involuntary whimpers of rising delight and need from her throat. Slowly he lowered his head to the slender column, his lips searing its length before they deliberately captured one pouting nipple, drawing it with relish into his mouth.

Never before in her life had Mistral known such intense, intoxicating sensations as she did now. Her head spun dizzily, as though she were drunk, and her body arched against him irrepressibly as he sucked her greedily, his tongue stabbing her with its heat, setting her on fire. Her limbs were as molten as the sweet rush of hot moisture that dampened her thighs, where an unbearable, burning ache that she instinctively yearned to quench had seized her.

Such were the turbulent emotions coursing wildly through her body that she was oblivious of Khalif's fingers trailing erotically down her rib cage, her stomach, to unfasten her blue jeans. With skill and assurance, he slipped his hand beneath the waistband of her panties to touch her where no man ever had before, eliciting from her a tiny mewl of sudden shock and dismay, mingled with uncontrollable, unmistakable pleasure as, lingeringly, he stroked the tender, mellifluous, swollen folds of her.

"Shh," Jordan murmured soothingly in her ear, silencing her soft cries with his mouth and shifting his weight so that his body half covered hers, stilling the restive, half frightened, half exhilarated movements that she had begun to make. "You're all ready for me, sweetheart. You want this just as much as I do. Let me show you that you do."

Then, so slowly and torturously that Mistral

thought that she would die from the blissful agony of it, he found the blossoming opening of her and pushed one finger deep inside of her, momentarily easing the sense of unendurable hollowness that gripped her, that sought intuitively to be filled. At his insidious invasion, she gasped with surprise and delight against his mouth, her lips softening and yielding pliantly to his plunging tongue, even as her thighs slackened and spread of their own accord for the encroachment of his hand below.

After a moment, a second finger joined the first, stretching her, opening her even wider for his onslaught. And then, as Khalif began inexorably to thrust his fingers in and out of her in an age-old rhythm designed to bring her to a feverish pitch, his thumb found the secret heart of her, rubbing the tiny nub tauntingly with each deep stroke.

In some dim corner of her mind, Mistral thought that she would be driven mad by the combination. Pleasure so fierce and excruciating that it took her breath away throbbed through her, focusing and heightening until it seemed that every nerve and muscle of her body was centered in that place that Khalif continued to fondle and stimulate. Surely she couldn't contain all of the volatile sensations that were building inside of her. Surely she would explode.

And then she did, and there was nothing that she could do except cling to Khalif tightly, crying out and calling his name as the tremors rocked her violently.

Afterward, kissing and caressing her, he slipped her sandals, blue jeans and panties from her, leaving her completely naked. Then he stripped off his own clothes. Mistral was hardly even cognizant of him sliding back into bed beside her, of his nudity. Her breathing labored, she lay still, shattered by the emotions roiling inside of her, the afterwaves of her climax, which pulsated through her.

"I didn't know that it would be like that," she whispered at last, swallowing hard.

"That's not the half of it, honey." Jordan took her in his arms once more, kissing her with a passion that left her head reeling, her body hungry again for whatever he had to offer. Still, when he began to enter her, she tensed—not much, but enough so that he was aware of it. "Trust me," he told her gently. "I won't hurt you, Mistral—at least, not any more than I have to, since I suspect that it's your first time."

"Does it show that much? How inexperienced I really am?" she asked softly, anxiously. "Did I—did I do something wrong, something that…displeased you?"

"No, not at all. But I gathered from Nicabar that you've never really had a serious relationship before, and I saw the expression on your face when Otto called me your boyfriend. So the odds were that you'd never taken a lover."

There *was* pain at first, but only a tiny twinge that soon dissipated once Khalif was fully inside of her. For a moment, he lay still atop her, accustoming her to the feel of him filling her, stretching and molding her to fit him. But then at last, he started to move, driving down into her strongly and deeply, and her body, awakened now to passion, stirred to life again, throbbing afresh with yearning for him.

Instinctively Mistral wrapped her long, graceful legs around him, enfolding him, arching her hips to receive each powerful thrust, and in that instant, she did not know where she ended and Khalif began. He swept her along with him to a primeval, mind-numbing place, where she was blind and deaf to all but him and the feelings that he aroused in her. Before she realized it, the explosive sensations had started to build inside her once more, burgeoning, bursting.

Khalif's mouth was on hers, his tongue mimicking the movements of his body as he plunged into her, bringing her swiftly to orgasm again, muting her cries of delight as the spasms overtook her, shook her down to the bone, making her buck and writhe beneath him, her head thrashing wildly. Then his own climax seized him, and he shuddered long and hard against her before he collapsed on top of her, his breath coming in harsh, uneven pants that mingled with her own labored breathing.

After a while, Khalif slowly withdrew from her, reluctant to leave her. He rolled onto his back, pulling Mistral into the cradle of his strong embrace, resting her head against his broad chest and stroking her long tawny hair tenderly. In her ear, she could hear the hard, rapid thudding of his heart, which matched her own, gradually slowing to a steadier pace. The fine black hair upon his chest felt like silk beneath her fingertips as, idly, she traced tiny circles there, marveling at the steely muscles that layered his torso.

Khalif was more than just the handsomest man whom she had ever seen, Mistral thought. He was beautiful, his body sculpted like that of some ancient, pagan god. She could scarcely believe that he was hers, that he loved her, that he wanted to marry her. Her heart swelled to overflowing with joy. Her own love for him had come upon her so swiftly and stealthily, taking her by such surprise, that she had not recognized it for what it was until he had spoken of his own feelings for her and compelled her to examine her heart.

But she *did* love him, she knew. She would not have slept with him otherwise, given to him the virginity that she had guarded so carefully for so long.

"Mistral, you never did actually answer my question about marrying me, you know," Jordan stated softly as they basked in the afterglow of their lovemaking, the sunlight and the summer breeze that filtered in through the open but lace-curtained windows of the trailer warm against their flesh. "But I assume that after what just passed between us, the reply is yes?"

"Yes...yes, it is," she breathed, glancing up at him and smiling tenderly. "I don't know why or how or even what the future holds in store for us, but I love you. I didn't want to, at first. Except for Nicabar, I've been alone for so long. I'd become so accustomed to looking out for myself that I think that I had grown more and more afraid of giving myself into someone else's keeping, of being forced to trust and depend on him. I...I still don't know how good I will be at that,

Khalif. So are you quite sure that marrying me is what you want to do?''

"Oh, yes. I don't have any doubts about that at all. And you will learn, in time, to trust me, to allow me to take care of you, Mistral, to know in your heart that you can always depend on me to be there for you. I promise you that.'' Because indeed, Jordan reflected, once she discovered who he really was, how much money he had, she would realize that she need never worry again that she would not be protected and cared for.

He should reveal to her his true identity, he recognized. And he would, Jordan promised himself— soon. But despite himself, he was unable to repress the twinge of guilt that he felt at the knowledge that he had deceived her, although he knew that there had been no malice in it, that he had not done it to hurt her.

"Do you—do you believe that Grandpapa will be pleased about our wedding, Khalif?'' Mistral inquired, pulling him from his reverie. "That he will give us his blessing?''

"I think that he would like nothing better,'' Jordan replied, smiling as he wondered if this was what had been in Nicabar's mind all along, the fact that his grandson and adopted granddaughter should fall in love. "Although I *don't* think that he would be happy about our sleeping together before we have been properly married.''

"Perhaps...perhaps, then, we ought not to have done so.'' Mistral bit her lower lip, torn with indecision. She did not want her grandfather to be disappointed in her.

"He may not even learn about it, and even if he does, he is a man of the world, my love. He will understand and forgive, even if he is old-fashioned and does not approve. And secretly, in his heart, he will think about great-grandchildren, and he will be glad that we have found each other. I believe that he despaired of my ever acquiring a wife—and I *know* that he feared that you would never find a husband to meet your high expectations."

"Well, if so, Grandpapa had no one to blame but himself—for it was he who always told me to set my sights on the moon." Mistral laughed gently at the memory.

"And now, you have chosen to settle for a lowly lion tamer instead." Jordan smiled, too, knowing that he teased her—although she did not yet share the joke. Or what he *hoped* that she would view as a very big joke, he thought, and not as an attempt to make a fool out of her.

"A lion tamer, maybe. But I would hardly call you lowly," she insisted.

"Perhaps not. After all, I succeeded in taming you, didn't I?"

"What? Did you think that I was a lioness?"

"At first. But now, I know that like Huseina, you are, despite all your feisty teeth and claws, only a pussycat at heart. And that being the case, I feel it's my job to make you purr again."

"And just what makes you believe that I will indeed 'purr'?" Mistral queried archly.

"This…and this…and this…" he murmured, his black eyes gleaming with triumph and satisfaction as he began to kiss and caress her once more in ways that swiftly aroused her desire anew and soon had her entreating him frantically for fulfillment.

Eleven

Intermission

Khalif had given Mistral an engagement ring—not a diamond, which she knew that he couldn't even begin to afford, but a beautiful ring with an old-fashioned, ornate gold setting. At its center was a huge, rectangular stone of green glass that glittered so gorgeously that she decided that it might have passed for an emerald to anyone who did not know better.

"I wanted something the color of your eyes," he had explained when he had slipped it onto her finger, and she had been deeply touched by that thought, by his gesture, the fact that he had bought a ring at all.

Many men in his position would not have. And

although Khalif was more well-off than a lot of circus performers, still, the cost of keeping up his lions and lionesses, their cages and his sixteen-wheeler was great. Despite that he had never said so, Mistral thought that he had had more than a few out-of-pocket expenses this summer, for which he had never requested the reimbursement that was his due.

It was difficult now to believe that she had ever doubted Khalif's loyalty, that she had ever once supposed that he was working for Bruno Grivaldi. For only a short while ago, they had discovered the true culprit behind all of the mishaps at the Big Top.

Otto had actually been the one to apprehend the miscreant—in the act of sabotaging the trapeze after having struck down Liam O'Halloran, their catcher, from behind, knocking him cold. To Mistral's horror, the malefactor had proved to be none other than Paolo Zambini! That was the true reason that he had taken to not being present to work her rope during the aerial ballet. He had been using that time to commit his acts of malice against the Big Top, aiding and abetting Bruno Grivaldi.

For the first time, Mistral had been unsure of herself, had not known what action to take. To think that Paolo had betrayed the Big Top in such a manner! Nicabar, too, had been in a state of shock. But Khalif had shown no hesitation or indecision whatsoever. He ordered Otto to restrain Paolo. Then he had telephoned an ambulance for the unconscious Liam and the police to arrest Paolo.

"I still can't believe it," Mistral said now, shaking

her head. "Paolo Zambini, of all people! And I had thought that it was Otto."

"Well, you were wrong," Deirdre said dryly as she dumped a tray of ice into the pitcher of lemonade that the two of them had just made together. "And thank God that you were. Otherwise, Liam would be lying in a morgue with a bashed-in skull—instead of having been sent home with only a mild concussion from the hospital."

"Oh, I know. I'm so glad that he's going to be all right! I nearly had a heart attack when I saw him lying there so still on the ground."

"You?" Deirdre exclaimed, shuddering. "I'm *still* shaking. My God. I thought that he was dead, Missy, and I'll never forget that hideous moment as long as I live. I believe that it took twenty years off my life."

"Well, try not to think about it anymore." Mistral patted her best friend's hand comfortingly. "Instead try to think about how we're going to manage the trapeze act tonight without Liam. Without a catcher, we can't perform—and the trapeze act has always been our grand finale. We could always just end the show with something else. But we're not far from Chicago, and this is the largest stadium that we play all year long. We just *can't* close without something big!"

"In that case, we should have trained somebody else ages ago who could take Liam's place," Deirdre observed, sighing heavily.

"Nobody else who was big and strong enough to act as the catcher would volunteer to learn, DeeDee.

You know that. You can't be afraid of heights and work the aerial acts like the trapeze.''

"So...what do you suggest, then?"

"I suggest that you allow me to take on the role of catcher,'' Jordan announced smoothly as he stepped inside of Mistral's trailer, the door banging shut behind him. "I haven't done it for a while, but it's just like riding a bicycle. Once you learn, you never forget how. After I repaired the trapeze cables that Paolo had damaged, I had some of the employees set up the equipment for the act. I've been practicing. I can still do it. However, whether you and DeeDee want to trust me to catch you is up to the two of you.''

The two women glanced at each other soberly.

"Khalif," Mistral said at last. "Are you—are you sure that you can do it? Because it's not that we don't trust you. It's not that at all. It's—it's the fact that the safety net isn't...well, it's old, and it isn't very sturdy anymore. I—I haven't ever told Grandpapa because he would have insisted on buying a new one...because of what happened to my parents, you see. And, well, we—we just couldn't afford the expense...''

"Do you mean to tell me that you all have been performing with a net that you knew wasn't safe?'' Jordan asked in a tone that made Mistral wince.

She hadn't seen Khalif so angry since the day that he had thought that Otto was threatening to hit her. Not even earlier today, when they had discovered that Paolo was the culprit working hand in glove with Bruno Grivaldi, had she seen Khalif so mad. His black eyes were narrowed, and a muscle flexed alarmingly in his taut jaw.

"Yes, but—" she began to reply, only to be rudely interrupted by him.

"We're not going to have any buts about this, Mistral. The trapeze act is canceled. Without a decent safety net, it's too dangerous, and I won't permit it."

"You won't permit it?" she parroted lamely. And then, without warning, her temper flared, and she flushed crimson with fury. "Oh, isn't that just like a man? You want to control everything! And I thought that you were different, Khalif! But now, I see that you're just the same—laying down the law as though DeeDee and I were children incapable of intelligently assessing the risks before us and making our own decisions. I won't have it, do you hear? I won't be treated that way—and if that's how you intend to behave, you can...you can just take your ring back and take a hike!"

Shaking from the force of her emotions, she wrenched off the engagement ring that he had given her and held it out to him, tears stinging her eyes.

"I don't want that," he insisted gruffly after a long moment. "Put it back on. I'll take care of the net some other way if you and DeeDee still want me to act as your catcher tonight."

"Fine." Mistral nodded tersely, her chin set at a pugnacious angle.

Jordan was furious at Mistral for the risks she'd taken to keep the Big Top going. He knew that if their grandfather had been aware of the condition of the safety net, he would have put a halt to the trapeze act immediately. And now, Jordan couldn't tell him, because Mistral would know that he had ratted on her, and then she might try to give his ring back again.

"I've got some calls to make," he said shortly. "I'll see you later."

"Whew." Deirdre heaved a sigh of relief after the lion tamer had left the trailer. "I don't know how you dared to stand up to him like that, Missy. I'd have been sick, thinking about throwing a man like that away. He's in love with you, you know, and he only wanted to protect you."

"I'm aware of that. But no matter how much he loves me—or that I love him, for that matter—I have to maintain some sort of independence, DeeDee. I simply refuse to be browbeaten like Otto's poor wife, Greta."

"I don't think that Khalif would ever treat you like that, Missy. He may be just a lion tamer, but there's something real classy about him all the same. Whatever else he may be, something tells me that Khalif Khan is a gentleman through and through."

Mistral sighed. "Oh, DeeDee, in my heart, I know that you're right. It's my head that's all mixed-up. Ever since I met that man, I've felt as though I got a stunning blow that has left me reeling."

Deirdre laughed at that. "Well, you did, Missy. You fell head over heels for him. That's what love is…one long, rambunctious tumbling act. Sometimes, you're up, and sometimes, you're down, and sometimes, you're just going around and around. It's dizzying, romantic, exciting, even infuriating at times. But one thing it never is, and that's boring."

"Do you ever get used to it, settle down at all?"

"Yes—eventually. But the truth is that, even now, my stomach still does flip-flops when Liam looks at me in a certain way." As Mistral blushed fiercely, Deirdre grinned knowingly. "Uh-huh. That's what I thought. So...was Khalif as good in bed as he looks as though he'd be?"

"Deirdre!"

Her best friend shrugged. "Well, it didn't hurt to ask—and after all, you *are* going to marry the man, which is the most wonderful news that I've heard in ages. Oh, Missy, I'm just so happy for you!" Deirdre thumped her now-empty lemonade glass down on the kitchen table to give Mistral a quick, warm hug, then stood. "I've got to go. Even though the doctors said that he's going to be fine, I don't want to leave Liam alone too long. See you later."

"Yes, all right."

After Deirdre had gone, Mistral slowly rose to clear the empty glasses off the table, then put the pitcher of lemonade in the icebox. What an eventful and upsetting day so far this one had turned out to be. With dismay, she wondered what else might happen. She wondered what in the hell Khalif thought that he could do about the safety net between now and tonight's performance.

Twelve

***

The Finale

It was not until after the show that Mistral finally understood how Khalif had been able to arrange and pay for a brand-new safety net to be delivered to the Big Top within hours after leaving her trailer.

The Spectacular Solanas, with Khalif as their catcher, having finished their act with an intricate series of flying passes and somersaults that had ended with Mistral and Deirdre on the same trapeze bar, took their bows to an enthusiastically cheering and applauding audience. Then they headed from the arena into the backstage area.

There, much to Mistral's startlement and confusion,

a horde of reporters awaited. There were a number of blindingly bright lights directed at the circus performers from cameras as photographers snapped pictures and broadcast journalists rolled tape. Microphones were shoved into the faces of Mistral and the rest, and reporters shouted out questions that, at first, she could not make heads nor tails of, not comprehending whom they were being asked of.

"Mr. Westcott, is there any truth to the rumor that you resigned as president of Westcott International three months ago?"

"Sir, what prompted you to assume an alias and become a circus performer?"

"Mr. Westcott, although even your late father never did anything quite this wild, would you say that you were following in his footsteps, even so?"

"Sir, who is running Westcott International in your prolonged absence?"

"Mr. Westcott, have the stockholders of Westcott International been informed that for the past three months, you have been performing as a lion tamer in a second-rate circus?"

"Sir, how do you respond to Mr. Bruno Grivaldi's accusations that your acquisition of his Jungle King Circus was a hostile takeover?"

"Mr. Westcott, have you taken leave of your senses?"

"Certainly not!" Jordan snapped heatedly in response to this last as he determinedly elbowed his way through the throng, dragging a thoroughly bewildered Mistral along in his wake. Finally, observing

with dismay the fact that he was not going to be able
to get through without making some kind of a statement to the media, he paused. "Ladies and gentlemen, I'd like to be brief if I may, since I will be
issuing a formal statement to the press just shortly. In
the meantime, let me just say that the Big Top Circus
is owned by my grandfather, Nicabar Danior. As I
had not seen him for quite a while and had several
weeks of leave from Westcott International due me,
I decided to spend my summer vacation performing
as a lion tamer for his circus. As some of you may
be aware, my mother, Sophia Danior Westcott, performed in this very same circus in her younger days.
It was where she met my late father. And as I had
many happy memories of the Big Top from my own
childhood and young manhood, it seemed only natural for me to lend my grandfather a helping hand.
Now, if you'll excuse me—"

"Mr. Westcott, who's the woman with you? You
seem quite attached to her, sir."

"That's because I am. Allow me to present my
fiancée, Ms. Mistral St. Michel. Now, please, I have
no further comment to offer at this time."

This wasn't happening. This wasn't real, Mistral
thought dazedly in some obscure corner of her mind.
This crowd of media people were talking to Khalif as
though he were somebody of consequence. They were
calling him *Mr. Westcott* and *sir*, in tones that were
such that they might have been addressing the president of the United States. One of the reporters had

even said something about him being a president—
the president of Westcott International.

Oh, God, Mistral thought suddenly, stunned,
stricken. Even she, so far removed from the floors of
Wall Street and big business, had heard of Westcott
International, global enterprise. They were involved,
among other industries, in shipping, manufacturing,
real estate and oil, she believed. And because she had
seen the huge, brightly lit *WI* on many of their towering buildings, she knew that they also owned a
chain of hotels worldwide, including a casino in At-
lantic City, and a couple of magazines, as well. *Oh,
God.*

Feeling as though she were caught up in some
dreadful nightmare, Mistral stumbled and nearly fell,
trying to keep up with Khalif's—*Mr. Westcott's,* she
corrected herself numbly—long stride as he pushed
open the stadium doors and hurried her across the
halogen-lit parking lot toward her trailer.

Once inside, Jordan sat her down firmly upon the
bed. Then, seeing how ashen her face was, he swore
softly but fiercely and began ripping open the cabinets
in her kitchen until he found a bottle of champagne
that he had brought to supper one evening. Mistral
had refused to open it, insisting that she could tell
from the elegant label that he had spent far more on
the bottle than he ought and that they would therefore
save it for a special occasion.

Deftly, Jordan popped the bottle's cork, cursing
again when Mistral flinched at the small explosion.
She didn't own any champagne flutes, so he was

forced to make do with a wineglass, into which he
poured the golden, bubbly alcohol before he joined
her on the bed.

"Here, you've had something of a shock, I fear.
Drink this. It ought to be brandy, and it isn't. But at
least it's better than nothing." He pressed the wineglass into her hand.

She sat there staring at the champagne dully, not
lifting the glass to her lips, despite his urging her to
drink up. Then, at last, she spoke, her tone wooden,
tightly controlled.

"You know, that night, when I said that the bottle
had an expensive-looking label on it, I was thinking
maybe ten…fifteen dollars, tops. Now, I'd be willing
to wager that this champagne cost more than I earn
in a week…maybe even a month."

"Does that really matter, Mistral?" Jordan asked.

"Yes, I think that it does. You…you tricked me,
Mr. Westcott. You made a complete fool out of me.
I—I realize, now, that I was never anything more to
you than just a—a summer fling—" She broke off
abruptly, biting her lower lip, an anxious habit that
Jordan had come to find terribly endearing.

But he winced visibly at being addressed by her as
"Mr. Westcott." "My first name is Jordan," he told
her gently. "And I assure you, sweetheart, that I am
definitely *not* in the habit of introducing a casual date
to the media as my fiancée or of having the Westcott
emeralds removed from the family safe in order to
give an engagement ring to a summer fling."

Mistral's slanted green eyes slowly widened with shock at that. Then she gasped audibly.

"You—you mean this—this is *real?*" she exclaimed, indicating her engagement ring, which she had until now thought was only a beautiful stone of green glass.

"Yeah, it's quite real."

For a long moment, she gazed at it, awed and marveling. Then, finally, her shoulders shaking with deep emotion, her hand trembling, she removed it from her finger and held it out to him.

Her voice was tremulous as she said quietly, "I— I thank you very much for the offer, Mr. Westcott, but I—I can't possibly accept it now. Before, when I thought that you were only a lion tamer—albeit a very good one—I knew that I was your equal. But now, I can only be ashamed at how inferior my station in life is compared to yours. I know that I don't have your background or education, that I couldn't possibly be a suitable wife for somebody like you. I couldn't even begin to fit into your world."

"You'll fit into my world just fine, honey," Jordan insisted firmly, taking the ring from her outstretched hand and deliberately pushing it back onto her finger. "Now, look here, Mistral. I know that this has all been a real shock to you...finding out that the man whom you're going to marry isn't a lion tamer at all, but, rather, the president of a worldwide company. But I sincerely hope that you'll forgive me for the deception. It was necessary to avoid exactly the sort of thing that happened tonight after the show. I can only assume that by now, Bruno Grivaldi has learned not only my identity, but also my whereabouts, that he was the one who sent the media here, in the hope of making me appear to have gone off my rocker."

"All of those reporters…they said something about your buying the Jungle King Circus," Mistral observed, as she suddenly remembered what the media had shouted at Jordan.

"Yeah, that's right. Bruno Grivaldi is an extremely unsavory character who is either at this very moment sitting in jail, along with Paolo Zambini, or who will be there shortly. The private investigators whom I hired to dig into his background uncovered enough dirt on him that he'll probably eventually be going away to prison for quite a long time. In the meanwhile, the Jungle King Circus was forced into receivership, and once that happened, I bought it out. So you don't have to worry that Grandpapa is going to lose the Big Top, Mistral. He won't, because I will, of course, require a competent manager for my new circus, and I intend to ask Grandpapa how he feels about combining the two circuses under the name Big Top and hiring a management staff to help him oversee the operation. I've been doing a lot of talking to Liam O'Halloran, and I thought that he and DeeDee might be interested in the job."

"Oh, Khalif…Jor-Jordan, you've considered everything, haven't you? A way to make everybody's dreams come true—except for mine."

"Sweetheart, you must know that as my wife, you can do pretty much anything that you want to do, whether it's running one of my magazines or decorating my hotels. I know that you love me. *Me*, Mistral. The person that I am inside. Not Jordan Anthony Westcott, president of Westcott International, multimillionaire, mover and shaker on a global scale. But just me. You don't know what that meant to me. All my life, I've always had to wonder whether people liked me for myself or because of who I was. It turned out that most of the women in my life were more attracted to my money than they were to me. But you didn't know who I was, Mistral. You didn't know anything about my background or wealth. Why, I don't believe that you even *liked* me that day when we first met—and you certainly didn't want anything from me."

"No...I thought that you were really working for Bruno Grivaldi and that you intended to displace me in Grandpapa's affections, besides." Mistral smiled wryly at the memory. "And all the time, you were his real grandchild, while I was only the adopted one."

"Grandpapa couldn't love you more if you *were* related to him by blood," Jordan assured her. "He was so happy to learn about us getting married. Please don't hurt and disappoint him now by turning me down, Mistral. Please don't hurt and disappoint *me*. I love you. I want you as my wife—and I warn you, I can be very persuasive and determined when I choose."

"You know, somehow, I don't doubt that in the least. But, oh, Jordan, are you—are you sure about this?" Mistral asked anxiously, unable to quite believe that the man whom she loved had turned out to be, in truth, not a lion tamer, but the president of Westcott International.

"I'm sure...very sure." He breathed a sigh of love and relief as, after a moment, she moved into the circle of his arms, lifting her face for his kiss.

"Then I suppose that I'll just have to marry you, after all," she said, her voice tremulous and husky with all of the love for him that welled inside of her. "I only hope that Huseina knows how to share!"

"Well, if she doesn't, then I'm afraid that she'll have to be permanently confined to her cage," Jordan declared, "because I've got the lioness I want right here."

Covering her mouth with his own, he pushed her down onto the mattress, kissing her fervidly as he did so, as though half-afraid that she wasn't truly real, that she hadn't actually agreed to wed him. Mistral whimpered low in her throat, inciting him, and the pressure of his lips increased, grew more demanding, until she was clutching him tightly and kissing him back wildly. Rolling across the bed together, they tore at each other's clothes, mouths and tongues and hands unstill as garments were discarded helter-skelter. Then, finally, the two of them lay naked together, flesh pressing flesh enticingly.

Mistral quivered with rapidly burgeoning desire and need as Jordan kissed and caressed her all over, his lips and hands lingering on her throat, her breasts, her belly, teasing and arousing her unbearably. Moaning, she writhed against him invitingly, ripples of electric delight radiating through her entire body. Her own mouth and hands explored him as eagerly and intimately as his did her, mapping every plane and angle of his hard, powerful body.

Then, before she realized what he intended, he spread her thighs wide, his lips finding the secret heart of her, driving her crazy. Never before in her life had Mistral known such heady, exquisite sensations as she did now. Her head reeled, as though she were intoxicated, and her body arched against Jordan irrepressibly as he slid first one finger, and then two, inside her, while, with his tongue, he stimulated the tiny nub that was the key to her rapture. Her mind seemed to spin away into nothingness, and her body was a mass of incredible, throbbing sensation, every nerve and muscle alive and screaming for an end to their sweet torture. Her hands reached down to tunnel through his hair, frantically pulling him even closer.

The unbridled emotions coursing rampantly through her body were such that Mistral felt as though she had lost all command of herself, was Jordan's to do with as he willed—and did—pleasuring and stroking her until her head was thrashing uncontrollably and she was desperately begging him for release. When at last it came, she gasped and cried out, gripped by such an intense spasm that she knew nothing but the waves of ecstasy that swept through her like a riptide, leaving her breathless and exhilarated.

Before she could gather her composure, Jordan lay atop her, his hard, pulsing sex finding and entering her in a single swift, deep stroke that made her keen aloud again with delight. With her long, graceful legs, she encircled his waist tightly. Her hips lifted ardently to meet each strong thrust as he drove into her over and over, faster and harder, taking her with him to an exquisite, soul-stirring place, where he filled her completely, urging her once more toward climax.

All the while, his mouth moved on hers fiercely, his tongue plunging as deep as he himself did, so that she seemed to be burning feverishly everywhere, molten and roiling, as though preparing to erupt. And then the explosion did come, bursting through her so forcefully that for an interminable, breathless moment, Mistral felt as though she would pass out. Jordan's own climax seized him then, and he shuddered violently against her before he collapsed atop her, panting and sweating, his heart thudding wildly against hers.

After a time, he withdrew, rolling to one side, cradling her tenderly against his chest, and stroking her hair idly.

"Mistral," he murmured, "I want to get married as soon as possible. As much as I love you and the circus, I don't think that I can take this narrow bed much longer."

"I suppose that you have a very grand bed," she said, glancing up at him wonderingly, as though still not quite able to believe that he was actually Jordan Anthony Westcott, multimillionaire, and no real lion tamer at all.

"Yes, as a matter of fact, I do—and we will not

only make love, but also several beautiful babies in it.''

"And what will Huseina say to that, I wonder?"

"Meow?" Jordan suggested, grinning.

"More like grrrrr, I imagine." Mistral smiled teasingly as she continued to gaze up at him, her eyes filled with love.

"And what do *you* say, my gorgeous lioness?"

"Purrrrr," she whispered throatily.

"Hmm. Me, too."

Epilogue

Encore

The reserved-seat tickets for the Big Top Circus were the best that money could buy, front and center for the show that was rumored to rival even the Ringling Bros. and Barnum & Bailey Circus. Uncle Charles and Sophia sat in two of the seats. The rest were occupied by Jordan and Mistral, their four-year-old daughter, Katie, and their two-year-old son, Rick. It was the children's very first visit to the circus, and they were so excited that their seats would hardly contain them.

Indulged by their doting father, they had already acquired T-shirts emblazoned with the Big Top logo,

dancing monkeys on sticks, stuffed replicas of Huseina and enough popcorn, peanuts and cotton candy
that Mistral expected one or the other of the children
to be sick at any moment. But when she had voiced
this concern aloud, Jordan had only laughed.

"That's part of going to the circus, sweetheart,"
he had declared.

Now, both of the children squealed with delight as
the clowns that warmed up the audience before the
show did their shtick, fashioning balloons into all
kinds of inventive shapes and creatures, then tossing
them up into the audience. Liam O'Halloran, winking
broadly as he clowned outrageously, a wild wig stuck
on his head, a big red bulb on his nose, and wearing
an oversize coat and shoes, made sure that Katie and
Rick each got one of the balloons.

"Mommy, wasn't that Uncle Liam?" Katie asked
afterward.

"Yes, darling. And Aunt DeeDee's the one with
that flaming orange hair and hideously flowered
dress."

"But I thought that she and Uncle Liam managed
the circus, along with Great-Grandpapa."

"Well, they do, but they still like to perform, too.
Oh, look, there's Grandpapa now."

The stadium lights abruptly dimmed, a bright white
spotlight highlighting Nicabar as, dressed in his traditional black top hat and tails, his red-satin-lined
cape and white gloves, he stepped into the center ring
and spread his arms wide.

"Ladies and gentlemen, boys and girls of all ages, welcome to the Big Top!"

"Do you wish that you were still a part of the circus, Mistal?" Jordan asked as he slid his arm around her, drawing her as close to him as the seats would allow.

"Sometimes," she admitted wistfully, then smiled. "But I wouldn't trade it for my life with you. Besides which, the new line of children's furniture and accessories that I've created is doing quite well, thank you very much. People have fallen in love with the Under the Big Top theme. I mean, what child wouldn't want to sleep in a crib resembling a lion cage or have a rocking horse decked out like the horses in a bareback-riding act?"

"I can't think of any. Certainly not our own. Look at the expressions on their faces. They've already fallen in love with Big Top, too."

"The same way that I fell in love with you," Mistral said softly, her eyes shining as, lifting her head from his shoulder, she gazed up at her handsome husband.

"And I, you." His arm tightened lovingly around her.

"Hey, you two lovebirds." Uncle Chas leaned across the children to address Jordan and Mistral. "Sophia and I have been talking, and, well, do you think that Nicabar would be interested in a clown act involving a runaway golf cart?"

"Oh, Chas, hush!" Sophia whispered, grinning and playfully swatting his arm in reproof. "Don't you dare laugh, you two, or otherwise encourage him," she told Jordan and Mistral. "There have been quite enough circus performers in this family as it is."

"Do you think that we should tell Mother that Katie's already asked for a trapeze bar for her birthday," Jordan inquired teasingly of Mistral, "and that Rick wants a lion-taming whip for his?"

"No." She shook her head, chuckling. "She'll find out soon enough. And besides, what's more, I'm very much afraid that the way this one's moving around—" she patted her stomach, swollen with her third pregnancy "—we've got a tumbler in the making, too!"

* * * * *

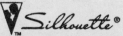

Take 2 bestselling love stories FREE

Plus get a FREE surprise gift!

Special Limited-Time Offer

Mail to Silhouette Reader Service™

> P.O. Box 609
> Fort Erie, Ontario
> L2A 5X3

YES! Please send me 2 free Silhouette Desire® novels and my free surprise gift. Then send me 6 brand-new novels every month, which I will receive months before they appear in bookstores. Bill me at the low price of $3.49 each plus 25¢ delivery and GST*. That's the complete price, and a saving of over 10% off the cover prices—quite a bargain! I understand that accepting the books and gift places me under no obligation ever to buy any books. I can always return a shipment and cancel at any time. Even if I never buy another book from Silhouette, the 2 free books and the surprise gift are mine to keep forever.

326 SEN CH7V

Name	(PLEASE PRINT)	
Address	Apt. No.	
City	Province	Postal Code

This offer is limited to one order per household and not valid to present Silhouette Desire® subscribers. *Terms and prices are subject to change without notice. Canadian residents will be charged applicable provincial taxes and GST.

CDES-98   ©1990 Harlequin Enterprises Limited

FOLLOW THAT BABY...

the fabulous cross-line series featuring the infamously wealthy Wentworth family...continues with:

THE DADDY AND THE BABY DOCTOR

by Kristin Morgan

(Romance, 11/98)

The search for the mysterious Sabrina Jensen pits a seasoned soldier—and single dad—against a tempting baby doctor who knows Sabrina's best-kept secret....

Available at your favorite retail outlet, only from

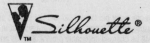

Silhouette ®

Look us up on-line at: http://www.romance.net

SSEFTB2

#1 *New York Times* bestselling author

NORA ROBERTS

**Presents a brand-new book in the
beloved MacGregor series:**

THE WINNING HAND
(SSE#1202)

October 1998 in

Silhouette ® SPECIAL EDITION ®

Innocent Darcy Wallace needs Mac Blade's protection in
the high-stakes world she's entered. But who will protect
Mac from the irresistible allure of this vulnerable beauty?

**Coming in March, the much-anticipated novel,
THE MacGREGOR GROOMS
Also, watch for the MacGregor stories
where it all began!**

**December 1998:
THE MacGREGORS: Serena—Caine**

**February 1999:
THE MacGREGORS: Alan—Grant**

**April 1999:
THE MacGREGORS: Daniel—Ian**

Available at your favorite retail outlet, only from

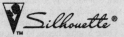

COMING NEXT MONTH